MW00950637

Table Of Contents

Introduction

Welcome to "Interesting Stories For Curious Kids," a book filled with amazing stories about history, science, pop culture, and so much more. This book is perfect for anyone who loves to learn new things and discover fun facts about the world. It is your ticket to explore and enjoy all sorts of interesting topics. It's designed to make you think, laugh, and wonder about all the cool and weird things that make our world so fascinating. So, grab this book and let's start exploring together!

The Chicken Who Didn't Need a Head to Have Fun

Once upon a time in the sunny state of Colorado, there was a chicken named Mike. But Mike wasn't just any chicken — he was special because he lived for 18 months without his head! Now, you might wonder, how could a chicken live without his head? Let's cluck into the story of Miracle Mike!

It all started in September 1945. Mike's owner, Farmer Lloyd, wanted to make a chicken dinner for his mother-in-law. He aimed to cut Mike's head off in just the right way, leaving a bit of the neck behind. But even though Farmer Lloyd did cut off Mike's head, something unbelievable happened — Mike didn't stop moving! Instead, he got up, shook it off, and kept on walking around like it was just another day in the yard.

Farmer Lloyd and his family were shocked. After watching Mike for a while and seeing that he wasn't giving up, they decided to help him out and see how long he could keep going like this. Farmer Lloyd fed Mike with a dropper, giving him water mixed with milk and tiny corn grains. He also used a little syringe to gently clean Mike's throat so he wouldn't get sick.

Mike turned into a real superstar! He traveled around with a show, where people came from far and wide to see the amazing headless chicken. He was even in big magazines, where everyone read about his strange but true story. They called him "Miracle Mike," and he showed everyone that even a chicken without a head can still have lots of pep and fun.

Now, you might be thinking, "How did Mike do all this?" Well, chickens have a special part at the base of their brain called the brainstem, which controls most of their basic activities, like walking and pecking. Lucky for Mike, the cut missed this vital spot, so he could keep on living a somewhat normal chicken life.

Mike's tale is more than just a funny chicken story; it shows us how strong and surprising nature can be. Mike kept on clucking without a head, reminding everyone that sometimes in life, you keep going no matter what strange twists and turns come your way.

So remember Mike the Headless Chicken as a feathered hero who didn't need a head to have fun and live life to the fullest. Even under the weirdest circumstances, you can still make the most of what you have and keep hopping along!

The Royal Tummy Trouble That Changed History

A long time ago, in the year 1135, there was a king named Henry I of England who had a very strange and rather embarrassing end. His story isn't just about a king but also about a meal of lampreys that led to a royal disaster!

King Henry I was a powerful king who loved to be in charge. He was known for being smart and stern, keeping his kingdom in order by making sure everyone followed his rules. But there was one thing Henry loved almost as much as ruling—eating lampreys. Lampreys are a type of fish, but not just any fish; they are long, slippery, and look a bit like eels. Not everyone thinks lampreys are tasty, but King Henry couldn't get enough of them!

One day, King Henry was visiting Normandy in France, where he decided to have a feast. At this feast, he ate a lot of his favorite dish—lampreys. Even though his doctors had warned him not to eat too many because they often made his stomach upset, Henry didn't listen. He thought, "What's the worst that could happen?"

Well, soon after the feast, the worst did happen. King Henry became very sick. His love for lampreys turned out to be his downfall because he got a terrible case of food poisoning. Back in those days, there weren't any modern medicines like we have now, so there wasn't much anyone could do once he became really ill.

King Henry's sudden sickness and death were a huge shock to everyone. Since he didn't have a son who was old enough to take over, his death led to a big fight over who should be the next ruler of England. This fight turned into a long and messy period called "The Anarchy," which lasted for many years as different people battled to be king or queen.

The story of King Henry I and his fatal meal of lampreys is one of those strange but true tales from history. It shows us how something as simple as ignoring advice about what to eat can lead to big, unexpected changes, like a whole country being thrown into chaos!

So, remember King Henry I and his lampreys as a lesson in why sometimes, it's really important to listen to good advice—and maybe to be a bit careful about what you eat!

When Fish Fall from the Sky: The Curious Case of Raining Fish

Imagine a sunny day suddenly turning into an astonishing spectacle where fish, instead of raindrops, start tumbling down from the sky! This might sound like a scene from a quirky fantasy movie, but it's a real phenomenon that has occurred in various parts of the world. Known as "raining fish," this unusual event has puzzled people for centuries and continues to be a topic of fascination and wonder.

Raining fish is a rare meteorological phenomenon that has been reported in countries including Honduras, Australia, and India. In Honduras, it is so common there's an annual festival called "Lluvia de Peces" (Rain of Fish), celebrated in the city of Yoro. Locals and visitors gather every year to witness and celebrate this bewildering natural occurrence.

So, how does it happen? How can fish possibly rain down from the sky? The explanation lies in the powerful dynamics of severe weather, particularly waterspouts. Waterspouts are tornadoes that form over water. Although they are less intense than most of their land counterparts, waterspouts can be quite powerful. They function like a giant vacuum cleaner over the water, sucking up fish and other sea creatures as they move over the ocean or lakes.

During a strong waterspout, fish and small aquatic animals that are near the surface of the water can be hoisted up into the storm's vortex. Once caught up in the waterspout, these fish are carried over land. As the waterspout loses energy and dissipates, whatever it had sucked up is dropped back to the ground, sometimes miles away from the original body of water. This results in the bewildering sight of fish raining from the sky, much to the surprise (or delight) of the people below.

Although the phenomenon primarily involves fish, there have been instances where frogs and even small aquatic mammals were reported to have rained from the sky, following similar meteorological conditions.

The phenomenon of raining fish is a striking reminder of the power and unpredictability of nature. It illustrates how meteorological phenomena, while often dangerous, can also be downright astonishing. For those who experience it, raining fish is an unforgettable spectacle—a story of the sky that, on rare occasions, decided to surprise the earth with a gift from the waters.

The Time We Wanted to Nuke the Moon

Believe it or not, there was a time when some people in America had a wild idea: to set off a nuclear bomb on the moon! Yes, you heard that right — they thought about making a big, bright explosion on the moon's surface. It sounds like something from a wacky cartoon, but it really did happen, or at least, it was planned.

Back in the 1950s, during a time when many countries were racing to be the best in space exploration, America had a plan called Project A119. The idea was pretty out there: they wanted to explode a nuclear bomb on the moon. Why, you might ask? They thought it would show how powerful and capable they were, especially compared to their main rival at the time, the Soviet Union, who were also planning big space missions.

The people behind Project A119 started thinking about what would happen if they actually did this. They hoped the explosion would be big enough to be seen from Earth with the naked eye. They thought this huge flash on the moon would surprise and impress people all over the world.

But it wasn't just for show. Scientists involved in the project were also curious about the dust and other stuff that would be kicked up by the explosion. They thought studying this moon dust could teach them more about the moon and outer space.

However, there were also big worries about this idea. What if it went wrong? The explosion could harm the moon's surface or create lots of space dust that might mess up other space missions. Plus, exploding a bomb on the moon could be seen as a very aggressive act by other countries, and it might make them upset or scared.

So, after a lot of thought and planning, the people in charge decided not to go ahead with Project A119. They realized it was too risky and not a very friendly thing to do to the moon, which has always been there to light up our night sky, not to be a target for bombs.

This wild plan to nuke the moon shows how sometimes, big ideas need to be thought through from all sides. It's important to think about the consequences of our actions, not just whether we can do something, but whether we should. It's a good reminder that sometimes the best choice is to leave things just as they are, especially when it comes to our beautiful moon!

Humans Versus Birds: The Strangest War of All Times

Once upon a time in Western Australia, a peculiar "war" took place, one unlike any battle you might find in history books. This was not a war between nations or rival groups, but rather a battle between humans and birds. Yes, you heard right—birds! The year was 1932, and the opponents were none other than the Australian military and a flock of surprisingly resilient emus.

The story begins after World War I, when many Australian veterans were given land by the government to take up farming in Western Australia. However, the transition from soldiers to farmers was challenging, especially during the economic hardships of the Great Depression. To add to the farmers' troubles, large flocks of emus, which are native to Australia and quite large birds, began invading the farmlands. The emus were attracted by the abundant crops, and they wreaked havoc on the wheat fields, damaging fences and devouring the harvest.

Desperate for a solution, the farmers appealed to the government for help. In response, the Minister of Defence decided to send in the military, equipped with soldiers armed with machine guns—the same that had been used in World War I. The hope was that a show of force would scare off the emus and protect the farmers' livelihoods. Thus, the "Great Emu War" commenced in November 1932.

Led by Major Meredith of the Royal Australian Artillery, the military devised a plan to tackle the emu problem. However, what seemed like a straightforward mission soon turned comically complicated. The emus, with their surprising speed and unpredictable running patterns, proved incredibly difficult targets. They scattered in all directions when shot at, and their thick feathers provided unexpected armor against the bullets.

The soldiers found themselves in an absurd game of cat and mouse, with the emus outmaneuvering them at every turn. After several days of fruitless attempts that expended hundreds of rounds of ammunition, Major Meredith was forced to withdraw his forces. By December, it was clear that the military intervention had failed. The emus had dispersed, and while some had fallen, the majority survived the skirmish unscathed.

The Great Emu War ended in a victory for the emus, leaving the soldiers bemused and the government embarrassed. This unusual conflict became a humorous anecdote in Australian history, often cited as an example of a well-intentioned plan gone amusingly awry.

In the end, the farmers resorted to building stronger fences and finding more effective, less dramatic ways to manage the wildlife that shared their land. The Great Emu War of 1932 remains a whimsical reminder of nature's unpredictability and humanity's occasional overestimation of its dominion over the wild.

Cows and Their Best Friends: A Moo-ving Tale of Friendship

Did you know that cows can have best friends? It might sound surprising, but these gentle giants are quite social and emotional animals, much like us! Scientists have discovered that cows are not only smart but also have strong feelings and form close relationships with other cows. This friendship helps them feel happy and relaxed, just like how we feel better when we're with our friends.

In various studies, researchers have observed how cows interact with each other in their herds. They found that cows often pair up with particular friends who they spend a lot of time with. These cow friends graze together, rest close to each other, and show signs of distress when they are separated. Just like humans, these friendships help cows feel secure and content.

One interesting study showed that when cows are with their best friends, their heart rates are lower, and they show fewer signs of stress. This is similar to how we might feel a sense of calm and safety when hanging out with our best friends. It turns out that having a buddy is just as important for cows as it is for people!

But why is friendship so important for cows? Cows are herd animals, which means they naturally live in groups and rely on each other for protection and social interaction. Being in a friendly group can make a big difference in a cow's life. It can affect everything from their mood to how well they eat and even how much milk they produce if they're dairy cows.

Farmers have noticed that cows with friends tend to be healthier and more productive. Because of this, some farmers try to keep cow friends together when moving them from one field to another or changing their environment. Keeping cow friends together can help them adjust to new situations more easily because they have the comfort of their buddy by their side.

This moo-ving discovery about cow friendships reminds us of the universal value of having friends. Whether you're a human, a cow, or any other creature, having friends can make life better and a little less scary. So, next time you see cows in a field, remember that they might just be hanging out with their best friends, enjoying the day together!

The Mariana Trench: The Deepest Place in the Ocean

Imagine a place so deep that if you could put the tallest mountain there, it would still be covered by ocean! That place is the Mariana Trench, the deepest part of all the world's oceans. It's located in the western Pacific Ocean, a mysterious and dark spot beneath the waves where few have ever traveled.

The Mariana Trench isn't just deep; it's like a narrow and long underwater canyon. It stretches more than 1,500 miles long and is more than 36,000 feet deep at its deepest point—that's almost seven miles down! If you stood at the bottom of the trench, you'd be under more water than you can imagine, and it would be really, really dark because sunlight can't reach that far down.

A long, long time ago, the Earth's outer shell, which is made up of big pieces called "plates," started moving. The Mariana Trench was created by one plate pushing underneath another one, a process called "subduction." This is how many deep ocean trenches are made, but the Mariana Trench is the deepest of them all.

Because it's so deep and dark, exploring the Mariana Trench is very tricky. Special submarines that can handle the huge pressure of the deep sea are needed to go down there. The first time people reached the very bottom was in 1960, and only a few people have been able to do it since then.

When scientists explore the Mariana Trench, they find strange and wonderful sea creatures that have adapted to live in such a deep, cold, and dark place. Some fish and creatures can glow in the dark, and there are even some kinds of tiny organisms that love the super-hot water near underwater volcanoes or vents.

Studying places like the Mariana Trench helps us understand more about our planet's oceans and the life forms that are so different from us. It also teaches us about Earth's history and how the landscape under the sea has changed over millions of years.

So, the next time you look at the ocean, just think about the Mariana Trench below the surface. It's like a hidden world, filled with secrets waiting to be discovered, showing us how amazing and mysterious our planet really is!

The Bear Who Became a Soldier

In the middle of a big, important war called World War II, a group of soldiers from Poland made a new, very unusual friend. His name was Wojtek, and he wasn't a person — he was a bear! Yes, a real, fluffy brown bear who ended up being one of the bravest soldiers in the army.

Wojtek's adventure started when he was just a tiny bear cub, found in Iran by Polish soldiers who were very far from home. They had been walking and fighting for a long time and missed their families. When they saw the lonely little bear, they decided to take care of him, just like a pet. They fed him condensed milk from an old vodka bottle, and as he grew, he started eating fruits, marmalade, honey, and even drinking coffee!

As Wojtek got bigger, he became more than just a pet; he was like a real soldier. He lived with the soldiers, slept in the tents, and even learned to salute with his paw! The soldiers loved Wojtek so much that they made him an official member of their army group. They gave him a soldier's hat and a special job too.

When the soldiers had to move heavy boxes of ammunition, Wojtek watched them and learned how to carry these heavy boxes all by himself. He was very strong and wanted to help his friends. During a big battle in Italy, Wojtek carried ammunition boxes just like the other soldiers. He never dropped them and worked just as hard as anyone else.

People were amazed to see a bear helping out in the war, and Wojtek quickly became famous. He was even on the news! After the war, Wojtek moved to Scotland with his soldier friends. He spent the rest of his life in a zoo, where he was visited by many people, including his old soldier friends who never forgot their bear buddy.

Wojtek's story teaches us about friendship and helping each other, no matter how different we are. The soldiers and Wojtek took care of each other and shared many adventures. Wojtek the Soldier Bear shows us that anyone, even a bear, can make a difference and be a hero. So, always remember, no matter how big or small, or even if you're a bear, you can be a friend and a helper too!

How Smartphones Made Gum Less Popular

Once upon a time, chewing gum was something nearly everyone did. You'd see people chewing gum while waiting for the bus, standing in line at the grocery store, or just walking down the street. But then, something big happened that made gum a little less popular — the arrival of the iPhone and other smartphones!

So, what do smartphones have to do with chewing gum? It's a funny story, but it all makes sense when you think about it. Back before everyone had a phone in their pocket, people used to chew gum to pass the time or keep their mouths busy while they were bored. If you were waiting in line or sitting on a bus with nothing to do, popping a piece of gum into your mouth was an easy way to make the time go by faster.

But then, along came the iPhone in 2007, and it changed everything. Suddenly, people had a fun and interesting gadget that could do all sorts of things. Instead of chewing gum, they could send texts, scroll through photos, play games, or watch videos. All these new things to do meant fewer people were buying and chewing gum.

Studies showed that as more people bought smartphones, gum sales started to drop. People just weren't as bored as they used to be because their smartphones kept them entertained. Instead of reaching for a stick of gum, they'd reach for their phones.

It wasn't just about being less bored, either. Smartphones made people more conscious about how they looked and acted in public. When you're taking a selfie or talking on a video call, you might not want to be chewing gum. Plus, smartphones can be pretty distracting, so much so that people often forget about gum altogether.

This story of the iPhone and gum sales is a great example of how new technology can change even the little things in life, like how often we chew gum. It shows us that when something new comes along, it can shake up habits and trends in ways we might not expect.

So next time you're out and about, and you see fewer people chewing gum, remember — it might just be because they're all busy looking at their phones!

Why 536 Was the Gloomiest Year Ever

Imagine a year so dark and cold that it felt like the sun had forgotten to shine. That year was 536, and believe it or not, it was probably the gloomiest year to be alive! It wasn't because of monsters or magic spells, but because of something really strange happening with the weather.

The year 536 was not like any year we know today. People woke up to skies that were dark and misty, not just for a day, but for the whole year! This was because enormous clouds of ash covered the sun, making it look like a faint, distant moon during the day. This strange darkness spread across many parts of the world, from Europe to Asia and the Middle East.

Now, you might be wondering, "What caused all that ash in the sky?" Historians and scientists think that it was probably a huge volcano that erupted, spewing ash high into the sky. This ash was so thick that it blocked out the sunlight, making it chilly and dark on the ground. Because of this, it was much colder than usual, and this sudden chill caused a lot of problems.

First, with less sunlight, crops couldn't grow well, which led to a big food shortage. People were hungry because their fields of wheat, corn, and other plants didn't get enough sun to grow properly. It was like having a winter that never wanted to end!

But that's not all. This cold and dark environment was also perfect for germs to spread, and in 541, just a few years after the skies turned dark, a terrible plague known as the Justinian Plague broke out. This sickness spread very quickly and made a lot of people very ill.

Imagine living in a year when it's always cold, you can hardly see the sun, there's not enough food, and everyone is getting sick. That's why many historians think that 536 was the worst year to be alive. It was a tough time, and it took many years for the world to feel normal again.

This spooky year teaches us how powerful nature can be and how it can change our lives in big ways. It also shows us how strong people had to be to get through such tough times. So, if you ever think you're having a bad day, just remember 536 and think, "Well, at least the sun came up today!"

The Man Who Survived A Rod Through His Brain

Once upon a time, there was a man named Phineas Gage who had one of the most astonishing stories you could imagine. It all happened in 1848 when Phineas was working on building a railroad in Vermont. He was a smart, hardworking foreman, known for being very careful and responsible. But one day, something truly unbelievable happened that changed his life forever.

Phineas was using a long, sharp iron rod to pack explosive powder into a hole. The idea was to blast away rock to make space for the railroad tracks.

Normally, this was safe if done correctly, but that day, something went wrong. The powder exploded with the iron rod still in the hole, and the rod shot out like a rocket — right through Phineas's head!

Now, you might think that's the end of Phineas Gage, but it wasn't. Phineas didn't just survive — he stood up, walked around, and even talked! The iron rod had gone in through his cheek, passed behind his eyeball, and came out through the top of his head. It was shocking, but Phineas was alive. He was taken to a doctor, and amazingly, he recovered physically pretty well despite losing one eye.

But the really interesting part of Phineas's story is what happened after the accident. Before the injury, he was known as a polite, hardworking, and calm man. After the accident, he started acting differently. He became more impulsive and had trouble making good decisions. This change made a lot of people curious about how the brain affects the way we behave.

Phineas Gage's story is famous because it was one of the first times doctors and scientists could see how physical changes in the brain could affect someone's personality. It helped start a whole new way of thinking about the brain and psychology.

For nearly 12 years after the accident, Phineas traveled around with his iron rod, showing it to curious people and telling his story. He even went to work at P.T. Barnum's American Museum in New York City for a while. Eventually, Phineas's health declined, and he passed away. But his story didn't end there. It's still told today in schools, books, and museums as a remarkable tale of survival and science.

Phineas Gage's adventure with the iron rod teaches us about the mysteries of the brain and how much there is to learn about how our minds work. It's a story that mixes a bit of history, science, and a whole lot of astonishment at what people can endure. So, the next time you think about how we all think and act, remember Phineas Gage and his incredible iron rod journey!

The Great London Beer Flood: A Sticky Situation

Once upon a time, back in 1814, a strange and unexpected disaster struck the city of London. It wasn't a fire or a storm, but something nobody could have guessed—a flood of beer! Yes, you heard it right, a massive wave of beer swept through the streets, and it's known as the London Beer Flood.

This bubbly tale begins at the Meux and Company Brewery, located in the busy St. Giles neighborhood of London. Inside the brewery was a huge vat, and I mean really huge! It held over 135,000 gallons of beer, which is enough to fill a small lake. One day, one of the metal hoops around this enormous vat snapped suddenly. At first, nothing happened, and the workers thought all was well. But oh, were they wrong!

A few hours later, the whole vat burst open, and like a scene from a wacky cartoon, it unleashed a tidal wave of beer that was over 15 feet high! The beer smashed through the walls of the brewery and poured out into the streets like a frothy river, sweeping along everything in its path.

Nearby houses were flooded, and in some places, the beer rose up to the first floor of buildings. People were swept off their feet, and the streets were filled with furniture, debris, and, of course, barrels and barrels of beer. It might sound funny to imagine a flood of beer, but it was actually quite dangerous and caused serious damage.

Eight people lost their lives in this unusual disaster. Some were trapped in their homes, and others were overcome by the beer itself. The brewery was located in a poor area where many families lived in basement rooms that quickly filled with beer, making it hard for them to escape.

After the flood, the brewery was taken to court, but the disaster was ruled to be an "Act of God," and they weren't held responsible. This meant that the families affected didn't get any help or money for the damage. However, the brewery did eventually have to pay a fine and make sure their vats were safer in the future.

The Great London Beer Flood is one of those strange but true stories from history. It reminds us that sometimes unexpected things can happen, and they can have big impacts on the people and places around them. So next time you hear someone talk about "having enough beer to fill a river," just remember the story of the London Beer Flood, and think about how that actually happened once upon a time in London!

The Year People Couldn't Stop Dancing

Once upon a time in 1518, in the city of Strasbourg (which was then part of the Holy Roman Empire), something very odd happened — a woman named Frau Troffea stepped outside her house and started dancing. But she didn't stop after a few minutes or even a few hours. She kept dancing for days! And what's even stranger? Other people started joining her, one by one, until there were hundreds of dancers!

This wasn't a dance party or a festival. These people couldn't stop dancing, even though they were exhausted, hurt, and didn't understand why they were dancing at all. This event became known as the Dancing Plague of 1518, and it's one of history's most bizarre mysteries.

So, why did everyone start dancing? Well, no one knows for sure. Some people think it might have been due to a medical condition that affected the brain. Others suggest it could have been caused by ergot, a toxic mold that grows on damp rye and produces effects similar to LSD. Maybe these people accidentally ate some rye bread contaminated with this mold and started hallucinating.

Imagine how it must have felt! Your feet shuffle and stomp as if they have a mind of their own. You're tired, your body aches, and yet you can't stop dancing. Historians say that some dancers even collapsed from exhaustion or injury, which shows just how extreme this event was.

The authorities in Strasbourg were just as confused and worried as the dancers. To try to solve the problem, they thought that maybe if they let the dancers keep dancing, they would eventually stop. So, they cleared open spaces and hired musicians to play, hoping the dancers would dance themselves out of their frenzy. Unfortunately, this didn't work, and the dancing continued for about a month.

The Dancing Plague of 1518 is a story that shows how strange and mysterious the world can be. It reminds us of the times when people didn’t understand as much about science and health as we do now. Stories like this can teach us about how people react to unexplained events and how they try to find solutions, even when they’re not really sure what’s going on.

So next time you hear music and feel like dancing, just remember the Dancing Plague and be glad that you can stop dancing whenever you want!

The Glass King: A Tale of Royal Fragility

Once upon a time in the 16th century, there lived a king who believed something very unusual about himself. His name was Charles VI of France, but he's famously known as the "Glass King" because he thought he was made of glass! Yes, you heard that right—glass, like the windows or a drinking cup!

King Charles VI ruled France, but he wasn't always an ordinary king. After ruling wisely for many years, he started having some problems with his mind. This made him think and believe things that weren't true. The strangest of these beliefs was that he was made of glass and could shatter into tiny pieces at any moment.

Because of this fear, King Charles took some extraordinary steps to protect himself. He had iron rods sewn into his clothes to keep himself from breaking if he accidentally bumped into something. Imagine wearing clothes with metal inside—walking around must have felt like being a knight in armor, all to keep from "breaking"!

King Charles was so worried about shattering that he would hardly move. He often stayed very still, avoiding hugs and careful not to make sudden moves. At court, people had to walk around him very carefully to make sure they didn't "crack" their king.

This belief might sound funny now, but back then, it was a big problem for the king and his kingdom. Being a ruler is a tough job, and thinking you are made of glass definitely doesn't make it any easier. His condition affected how he led his country and made decisions, as you can imagine how tough it must be trying to run a country if you're afraid of breaking into pieces!

The story of the Glass King is one of the earliest recorded cases of what we might now call a mental illness, particularly a delusion. It helps us understand how mental health issues have been part of human history for a long time. It also shows us that everyone, even a king, can have challenges and needs understanding and support.

So, the tale of the Glass King isn't just a quirky story from history; it's a reminder of how important it is to take care of our minds and help others who might be going through tough times with their thoughts and feelings. Just like the fragile Glass King, a little care and support can keep us all from feeling like we're on the verge of breaking.

The Man Who Prevented World War III

Have you ever heard of Stanislav Petrov? Probably not, but he's a real-life hero who might have saved the world from a huge disaster. Back in 1983, during a tense time called the Cold War when two big countries, the United States and the Soviet Union, were not getting along, Stanislav did something very brave and very wise.

Stanislav was a lieutenant colonel in the Soviet Air Defense Forces. One night, while he was on duty, the computers that watched for missiles said that the United States had launched missiles at the Soviet Union. This was very serious because it could mean the start of a big, scary war — maybe even World War III.

Now, Stanislav had a huge decision to make. The computers were telling him that missiles were coming, and everything he learned in his job said he should tell his bosses so they could launch missiles back at the United States. But Stanislav had a feeling something was not right. The computers showed only a few missiles, which didn't make sense because in a real attack, he expected there would be many, many more.

So, instead of panicking or just following the computer's warning, Stanislav thought carefully and decided it must be a mistake. He chose not to report the missiles as a real attack. And guess what? He was right! It turned out to be a false alarm caused by the computers making a mistake with reflections of sunlight on clouds.

Because of Stanislav's calm thinking and brave decision not to react right away, he prevented what could have been a terrible war. His actions show us how important it is to stay calm in tough situations and to think carefully before making big decisions.

Stanislav Petrov might not be as famous as superheroes in movies, but he's a real hero who had the courage to trust his judgment and save the world from a possible disaster. So next time you think about heroes, remember Stanislav Petrov, the man who was brave enough to stop a war before it could start!

The Tale of the Too-Hot Coffee and a Big Court Case

Once upon a time in 1992, there was a famous court case that got a lot of people talking. It all started with a simple cup of coffee from McDonald's, but it turned into a big discussion about safety and responsibility. This is the story of the McDonald's Hot Coffee Lawsuit.

One morning, a lady named Stella Liebeck ordered a cup of coffee through the drive-thru at a McDonald's in Albuquerque, New Mexico. Stella was 79 years old and liked her coffee hot, just like many people do. But on this day, the coffee wasn’t just hot; it was super hot. McDonald's used to serve their coffee at a temperature between 180 to 190 degrees Fahrenheit, which is hot enough to cause a serious burn in just a few seconds.

While sitting in the passenger seat of her grandson's car, which was parked, Stella tried to add some cream and sugar to her coffee. Unfortunately, the cup tipped over onto her lap, pouring all the scalding hot coffee on her. She got very badly burned and needed to be taken to the hospital right away.

Stella spent eight days in the hospital and underwent several skin grafts to treat her third-degree burns. It was a painful and scary time for her. When she got better, Stella asked McDonald's to help pay for her medical bills, which were over $10,000. At first, she only wanted a bit of help, but McDonald's didn't want to pay what she asked for. So, Stella decided to take McDonald's to court.

The case went to trial, and a lot of people were surprised to learn that McDonald's coffee was so hot. The jury found out that Stella wasn't the only one who had been burned by McDonald's coffee; there were over 700 other cases before hers! In the end, the jury decided that McDonald's should have warned their customers more clearly about the dangers of such hot coffee.

The jury awarded Stella nearly $3 million, but that amount was later reduced by a judge. Even though the case was serious, some people made fun of it and thought it was just about someone suing over spilled coffee. But it was really about much more than that. It was about how companies need to make sure their products are safe for everyone and that they warn people about possible dangers.

Stella's case made a lot of companies think harder about how they serve their products and helped make things safer for all of us. It's a reminder that sometimes, even a simple cup of coffee can lead to big changes.

The Curious Journey of Einstein's Brain

Albert Einstein, the famous scientist who came up with the theory of relativity, was known for his brilliant contributions to science. But did you know that after he passed away in 1955, his brain went on an unexpected adventure? Yes, that's right—Einstein's brain took a strange and fascinating journey that puzzled and intrigued people all over the world.

When Einstein died, he wanted his body to be cremated and his ashes scattered in a secret location, which is what happened. However, he didn't say anything about his brain! A pathologist named Thomas Harvey, who was at the hospital where Einstein passed away, had other ideas. Dr. Harvey decided to keep Einstein's brain for research. He thought that by studying the brain of a genius, scientists might learn what made it so special.

Without permission from Einstein's family, Dr. Harvey removed the brain during the autopsy and took it with him. He later got approval from Einstein's son, but only after the fact. Dr. Harvey divided the brain into 240 pieces and kept them in jars of formaldehyde, which is a kind of preservative. Then, he began sending pieces of Einstein's brain to various scientists around the world.

For many years, Einstein's brain traveled more than Einstein himself had! It was studied by different researchers who were eager to find out what made this brain capable of such profound thoughts.

However, despite all this research, scientists didn't find anything that could definitively explain Einstein's genius. His brain looked mostly like anyone else's, with only slight differences in certain areas.

Dr. Harvey kept some pieces of the brain in his personal possession for decades. At times, he even took the brain with him in the trunk of his car as he moved from one place to another! It wasn't until the late 1990s that he returned what was left of the brain to Princeton Hospital, where Einstein had worked.

The story of Einstein's brain raises many questions about ethics and respect for people's wishes after they die. It also shows how curious humans are about understanding genius and the lengths they will go to uncover its mysteries.

So, the next time you learn something new or solve a difficult problem, think about Einstein and the incredible journey his brain took, all in the name of science!

The Story of the Most Kissed Girl in the World

Believe it or not, there's a fascinating story about a girl who has been kissed more than anyone else in the world, but it's not what you might think! This isn't a tale of a famous movie star or a princess but rather a mysterious young lady known as the CPR doll, or "Resusci Anne."

The story begins in the late 19th century in Paris, where the body of an unidentified young woman was pulled out of the River Seine. It was believed that she had drowned, but because she was never identified, the mystery of who she was and her story captivated many people. Her serene expression and enigmatic smile gave her an almost peaceful demeanor, as if she were simply asleep.

At the morgue, the pathologist was so struck by her beauty and peaceful expression that he ordered a plaster cast of her face. This cast, or death mask, soon became a curious art piece, displayed in homes and shops throughout Paris. Many artists were inspired by her mysterious allure, and she became a sort of muse for the bohemian culture of the time.

Fast forward to the mid-20th century, when a Norwegian toy maker named Asmund Laerdal was about to create something new. Asmund had already been successful with his innovations in soft plastics, which he used to make realistic-looking toys. When he was asked to develop a training tool for newly discovered CPR techniques, he remembered the hauntingly beautiful death mask of the unknown woman from the Seine.

Inspired, he decided to model the face of the first CPR training mannequin after her. He named this mannequin "Resusci Anne," and she became the face through which millions of people have learned lifesaving CPR techniques. Those practicing CPR techniques perform mouth-to-mouth resuscitation on Resusci Anne, effectively "kissing" her to practice saving lives.

Thus, Resusci Anne has been dubbed "the most kissed girl in the world," as countless students and professionals in over 100 countries have practiced lifesaving techniques on her. Her face, replicated from that mysterious girl who met such a tragic fate, has helped teach vital skills that have saved real lives.

So, while the identity of the original girl remains a mystery, her legacy lives on in a way she could never have imagined—by helping people learn to save others. It's a poignant reminder of how beauty and tragedy can intertwine and how legacy can emerge from the most unexpected places.

The Story of the World's Slowest Marathon Runner

Once upon a time, there was a marathon runner unlike any other. This isn't a tale of the fastest, the strongest, or the most athletic, but it's a special story about the world's slowest marathon runner, Shizo Kanakuri. His marathon story is so unique it might just change the way you think about winning and losing.

Shizo Kanakuri was a talented runner from Japan who was selected to compete in the 1912 Stockholm Olympics. It was a big honor and an even bigger adventure, as the journey from Japan to Sweden was long and exhausting. By the time Shizo arrived in Stockholm, he was tired and wasn't feeling his best, but he was determined to run the marathon.

On the day of the race, things didn't go as planned. The weather was much hotter than Shizo was used to, and he wasn't in the best shape after his long journey. During the marathon, he struggled more and more with each mile. Eventually, feeling overwhelmed by the heat and exhaustion, Shizo did something most unexpected—he stopped at a garden party along the marathon route and decided to rest.

However, Shizo didn't just rest for a few hours. He was so worn out that he fell asleep and ended up staying much longer than he intended. In fact, Shizo was so embarrassed and disappointed by his performance that he didn't even tell the race officials he was dropping out; he just went straight back to Japan!

For years, the Olympic organizers didn't know what had happened to Shizo. In their records, he was listed as a "missing" runner. Then, in a surprising twist, in 1967, Swedish television decided to create a documentary about the mystery of the missing marathon runner. They invited Shizo back to Sweden to finish his race.

Shizo accepted the invitation, and at 76 years old, he completed his marathon, finishing with a time of about 54 years, 8 months, 6 days, 5 hours, 32 minutes, and 20.379 seconds—making him the world's slowest marathon runner! His finish line was the same place where the garden party had been held all those years ago.

Shizo's story teaches us that it's never too late to finish what you've started, and sometimes, it's not about how fast you go, but about the journey you take and the courage to complete it. Shizo might have been the slowest, but he remains a beloved figure in marathon history, remembered not for speed, but for his endurance and spirit.

The Exploding Cigar: A Puzzling Plot to Stop Castro

Once upon a time during the Cold War, when spies and secret plots were more common than superheroes in comic books, there was a particularly unusual plan to stop a famous leader. This wasn't just any plan—it involved an exploding cigar, and the target was Fidel Castro, the leader of Cuba!

Fidel Castro came to power in 1959 and quickly became known for his fiery speeches and strong leadership in Cuba. However, not everyone was a fan of Castro, especially some folks in the United States. They were worried about his close ties with the Soviet Union and his communist government being so close to American shores. So, they came up with all sorts of plans to try to stop him.

One of the most bizarre ideas was the exploding cigar. The plan was simple but sounds like something out of a cartoon or a spy movie. The idea was to sneak a cigar filled with explosives into Castro's collection. When Castro lit the cigar—BOOM!—it would explode. It sounds crazy, but back then, ideas like this were taken quite seriously.

The CIA, which is the United States' Central Intelligence Agency, was tasked with coming up with ways to remove threats to America, and they had a whole program with various plots to undermine or get rid of Castro. The exploding cigar was just one of many ideas, including poisoned pens and other wild schemes.

However, like many plans in spy stories, the exploding cigar never actually reached Castro. He continued to lead Cuba for many decades, outliving many of the leaders who had once plotted against him. Castro was well aware of these attempts on his life and often joked about them in his speeches, showing that he wasn't easy to frighten or fool.

The story of the exploding cigar is a reminder of how intense and strange international politics can get. It shows us how creative (and sometimes downright odd) humans can be when they feel threatened or are in conflict. While it might sound funny to us now, at the time, it was a serious attempt to change the course of history.

So, next time you hear about a spy story or a secret plot, remember the tale of the exploding cigar—it's a perfect example of how truth can sometimes be stranger, and more explosive, than fiction!

The Man Struck by Lightning Seven Times

Imagine being struck by lightning not just once, but seven times! Sounds unbelievable, right? Well, there was a man named Roy Sullivan who experienced this shocking phenomenon. Roy was a park ranger at Shenandoah National Park in Virginia, USA, and he earned a nickname that sounds like a superhero: "The Human Lightning Rod."

Roy Sullivan was born in 1912 and spent most of his life working outdoors, which might explain some of his encounters with lightning. However, surviving seven lightning strikes is something truly extraordinary and made Roy quite famous.

The Seven Strikes

1. **First Strike:** In 1942, while Roy was in a fire lookout tower, lightning struck the tower. The tower was well-equipped with lightning rods, but somehow, the lightning found Roy. It burned a half-inch strip all along his right leg, hit his toe, and left a hole in his shoe!
2. **Second Strike:** In 1969, while driving his truck, another bolt struck. This time, it knocked Roy unconscious, burned off his eyebrows, and set his hair on fire.
3. **Third Strike:** A year later, in 1970, Roy was struck again in his front yard. The lightning hit his shoulder, searing it.
4. **Fourth Strike:** In 1972, while working inside a ranger station, another strike came down the chimney, setting Roy's hair on fire again!
5. **Fifth Strike:** In 1973, a storm caught him out in the open. Roy tried to run away, but the lightning followed, setting his hair on fire for the third time and knocking him out of his shoe.
6. **Sixth Strike:** In 1976, Roy saw a cloud he thought was following him. He tried to outrun it but was struck, injuring his ankle.
7. **Seventh Strike:** The final strike in 1977 happened when he was fishing. Lightning hit the water and traveled up the line, hitting him on the head. This strike sent him to the hospital with chest and stomach burns.

It's hard to say exactly why Roy Sullivan was hit by lightning so many times. Some people believe that certain factors like body chemistry or location might make a person more susceptible to lightning. Roy himself wondered if some force was trying to destroy him or if he just had an unusual ability to attract lightning.

Despite the dangers he faced, Roy continued his job as a park ranger until he retired in 1979. He always kept his sense of humor, joking that he could light cigarettes off his radiator when his car wouldn't start because of the residual electricity in his body.

Roy Sullivan's story is not only a record-breaking tale but also a reminder of the incredible power of nature and the resilience of the human spirit. His life shows that even after facing great challenges, one can continue with courage and humor.

The Apple That Inspired a Genius

Long ago in the 17th century, a young man named Isaac Newton made a discovery that would change the way we understand the world. Newton was not only a brilliant mathematician and physicist but also someone with a curious mind, always eager to solve the mysteries of nature. His most famous moment, which involves a simple apple, has become one of the most popular stories in the history of science.

Isaac Newton was born in 1643 in a small English village. As a young student, Newton was fascinated by the natural world, and he would often think deeply about the forces that make things move and stay in place. But it wasn't until one quiet afternoon in 1666, while sitting in his garden, that Newton had his big eureka moment.

According to the story, Newton was sitting under an apple tree when an apple fell and hit him on the head. This seemingly ordinary event sparked a groundbreaking thought in Newton's mind. He began wondering why the apple fell straight down, instead of going sideways or even up. This simple question led him to develop the law of universal gravitation.

Newton realized that there must be a force pulling the apple towards the earth, and he proposed that this same force also keeps the moon in orbit around the earth and the planets orbiting the sun. He called this force gravity, and he described it in his famous law: every particle in the universe attracts every other particle with a force that is proportional to the product of their masses and inversely proportional to the square of the distance between their centers.

This discovery was one of the key moments that contributed to the scientific revolution of the 17th century. Newton's laws of motion and his theory of gravity laid the foundation for classical mechanics, which scientists still use to describe the motion of objects from particles to planets.

Newton's curiosity and his willingness to question everyday occurrences led to discoveries that explained not just why apples fall from trees, but also how the universe behaves. His work shows us the power of asking why things happen and seeking answers through observation and reasoning.

So, the next time you see an apple fall from a tree, remember Isaac Newton and the afternoon that changed science forever. It's a reminder of how important it is to stay curious and to keep looking for answers, no matter how simple the questions may seem!

When America Said No to Booze

Once upon a time in America, there was a period known as Prohibition, when making, selling, and drinking alcohol was against the law. This time lasted from 1920 to 1933, and it was meant to solve problems caused by alcohol, like crime and health issues. However, instead of solving problems, Prohibition created a whole bunch of new and unexpected ones!

Prohibition started with the best intentions. Many people believed that alcohol was causing too much trouble in society. They thought that banning it would make America healthier and safer. So, in 1920, the United States introduced the 18th Amendment, which made it illegal to produce, sell, or transport alcoholic beverages.

But not everyone was happy with this new law. Many people still wanted to drink, and they were going to find ways to get alcohol no matter what. This led to the rise of secret bars called "speakeasies." Speakeasies were hidden clubs where people could go to enjoy music, dance, and, of course, drink illegally. To enter a speakeasy, you often needed a password, which made going out for a drink seem like an exciting adventure.

However, with the legal production of alcohol shut down, a dangerous black market sprang up. This market was controlled by criminal gangs who made their own alcohol, known as "bootleg" liquor. Since this alcohol wasn't regulated, it was often unsafe. Some of it was made with toxic ingredients that could make people very sick, or even cause death.

The government tried to enforce Prohibition by using "Prohibition agents," but there were not enough agents to control the massive illegal alcohol trade. This period saw a rise in crime and violence as gangs fought over control of the lucrative bootlegging business.

One of the darkest aspects of Prohibition was the government's decision to poison industrial alcohol—which was still legal for some uses, hoping to deter people from drinking it. Unfortunately, many bootleggers stole this alcohol, redistilled it, and sold it anyway. As a result, it's estimated that around 10,000 people died from drinking poisoned alcohol during Prohibition.

In 1933, America realized that Prohibition might have caused more problems than it solved. The 21st Amendment was passed, which repealed the 18th Amendment and ended Prohibition. People could legally buy and drink alcohol again, but the era had left a lasting mark on American society.

Prohibition taught a valuable lesson: banning something that many people want can lead to unintended and sometimes dangerous consequences. It's a chapter of history that reminds us of the complexity of social issues and the challenges of regulating human behavior.

The Mysterious Nazi Expedition to Antarctica

Long ago, in the late 1930s, a strange and secretive mission took place that sounds like something out of an adventure novel. The protagonists were Nazi explorers, and their destination was none other than the icy and mysterious continent of Antarctica. This mission, known as the New Swabia Expedition, has sparked curiosity and wild theories ever since.

In 1938, just before the world was plunged into the chaos of World War II, Nazi Germany sent an expedition to Antarctica. The official reason for this mission was to explore and possibly establish a whaling station, which would help Germany produce more fat for oil production—something crucial for any country gearing up for war. But, as with many things the Nazis did, there were layers of secrecy and possibly other motives behind their journey to one of the coldest, most remote places on Earth.

The expedition was led by Captain Alfred Ritscher, and the team used a ship called the MS Schwabenland. The ship was equipped with a catapult system that launched seaplanes, which were used to scout vast areas of the Antarctic territory. These planes flew over parts of Antarctica, taking thousands of aerial photographs and dropping Nazi flags to claim the land, which they named New Swabia.

While the official goal was exploring and scouting for a whaling base, there are many who believe that the Nazis had more secretive motives. Some theories suggest they were searching for a place to establish a secret base or were on a quest to find rare minerals or even seeking out a lost ancient civilization. These theories have been fueled by the Nazis' well-known interest in the occult and mysterious sources of power.

However, despite all the speculation, there is no concrete evidence that the Nazis built anything permanent or found anything particularly unusual in Antarctica. The onset of World War II soon after the expedition meant that any further plans were likely scrapped, as the Nazis turned their focus to the war effort.

The New Swabia Expedition remains a fascinating footnote in history, illustrating the lengths to which the Nazi regime would go to further their goals. It's a reminder of how geopolitical ambitions can extend to even the most inhospitable parts of our planet. This expedition to the icy south adds an intriguing layer to the complex narrative of World War II and continues to spark the imaginations of historians, conspiracy theorists, and adventure fans alike.

Unsinkable Sam: The Cat with Nine Lives at Sea

Once upon a time, during the turmoil of World War II, there lived a cat named Sam, who became known as "Unsinkable Sam." This wasn't just any ordinary cat—Sam had an incredible tale of survival that made him a legendary figure in maritime history. His story begins on a German battleship, but it doesn't end there, as Sam would sail on not one, but three different ships during the war!

Sam started his seafaring life as "Oscar," the mascot of the German battleship Bismarck. In May 1941, during a fierce battle in the icy waters of the North Atlantic, the Bismarck was struck by torpedoes from the British navy. As the ship sank, Oscar found himself in the cold ocean, struggling to survive. By a stroke of luck, he was rescued by a crew from the British destroyer HMS Cossack. Oscar, the German ship's cat, was now aboard a British ship, and his name was changed to Sam.

But Sam's adventures at sea were far from over. Only a few months later, the Cossack was also torpedoed. Sam found himself once again fighting for survival in the open ocean. Miraculously, he was rescued again, this time by the crew of the aircraft carrier HMS Ark Royal. Surely, by now, Sam must have thought his days of dodging torpedoes were over.

However, fate had one more twist in store. Not long after Sam's rescue, the Ark Royal was torpedoed too!

Once again, Sam was found clinging to a floating plank, seemingly unbothered by the chaos around him. He was rescued for a third time and returned to the shores of Gibraltar.

After surviving three sinking ships, Sam was declared "Unsinkable Sam" and decided that he had had enough of the high seas. He was sent to live out his days in a seaman's home in Belfast, where he became a beloved figure, basking in the warmth of a cozy fire rather than braving the cold ocean.

Unsinkable Sam's remarkable story of survival against all odds has made him an enduring symbol of resilience and luck. He is remembered not only as a mascot who brought comfort and morale to sailors during the war but also as a cat who refused to let the sea claim him. Sam truly lived up to the saying that a cat has nine lives, each one as thrilling as the last!

André the Giant: The Gentle Giant's Final Bow

In the world of professional wrestling and pop culture, few figures loom as large, both literally and figuratively, as André the Giant. Born André René Roussimoff in France in 1946, he grew to be over 7 feet tall and weighed 520 pounds due to a condition called acromegaly, which causes excessive growth. But it wasn't just his size that made him a legend; it was his enormous heart, gentle demeanor, and unforgettable presence that endeared him to millions around the world.

André's wrestling career skyrocketed in the 1970s and 1980s, making him one of the biggest stars in the World Wrestling Federation (now WWE). Known as "The Eighth Wonder of the World," André captivated audiences with his immense size and strength. Beyond the ring, he was loved for his kindness, sense of humor, and the legendary tales of his eating and drinking escapades.

Despite his larger-than-life persona, André faced significant challenges because of his size. His health began to deteriorate, burdened by his giant frame and compounded by wrestling injuries. Mobility became difficult, and the pain he endured grew worse over time.

In the late 1980s, André's health declined further, prompting him to step back from wrestling and explore acting. He found success and new fans with his role as Fezzik in "The Princess Bride," showcasing his lovable nature on the big screen.

Unfortunately, André's health issues caught up with him. On January 27, 1993, while in Paris for his father's funeral, André passed away in his sleep due to congestive heart failure. He was only 46 years old. His death marked the end of an era, but not without a peculiar twist typical of his larger-than-life story.

Given André's immense size, his family faced an unusual dilemma: When no crematorium in France was big enough for the task, his body had to be flown back to the United States. This unexpected hiccup added a strangely humorous note to the somber task of laying the giant to rest, reflecting the extraordinary life he led—one that often grappled with the practicalities of the world not built for someone of his stature.

André the Giant's legacy endures, remembered not only in wrestling circles but also by anyone who admired his character and warmth. He remains a cultural icon, a figure of immense physical power and an even greater heart, whose life story reminds us that greatness comes in many sizes and that kindness is the mightiest force of all.

The Teenager Who Sued His Own Mother

Once upon a time, not too long ago, there was a surprising story that made headlines and raised quite a few eyebrows. This tale comes from Spain and involves a teenager who did something most unusual—he sued his own mother! But before you jump to conclusions, let's dive into the details of this quirky court case.

The story begins with a 15-year-old boy from Andalusia, Spain, who found himself at odds with his mother over something many kids and teens can relate to: chores. Yes, chores—the everyday tasks like cleaning your room, taking out the trash, and helping around the house. It seems this teen was not too keen on these daily duties, and his mother was quite strict about them.

Feeling that his personal freedom was being infringed upon by his mother's insistence on chores and good behavior, the young man decided to take a step that most would consider extreme. He sued his mom, claiming that she was coercing him into performing tasks and that her methods of discipline were too harsh. The case actually went to court, which is quite unusual for family disagreements about household chores!

The courtroom must have been an interesting scene as the judge listened to the case of the teen versus his mom. After hearing both sides, the judge made a decision. He ruled in favor of the mother, stating that her methods were reasonable and that it was perfectly within her rights to expect her son to contribute to household chores and maintain good behavior at home.

The judge's decision emphasized that parents have not only the right but also the obligation to take care of their children, which includes setting rules and expectations. The ruling supported the idea that chores and responsibilities are part of growing up and becoming a responsible individual.

This curious case from Spain serves as a humorous yet thought-provoking reminder of the conflicts that can arise between parents and children. It highlights the challenges of parenting and the sometimes amusing lengths to which disagreements can go. So next time you find yourself grumbling about doing the dishes or cleaning your room, remember the tale of the Spanish teen who sued his mom over chores—and think twice about taking your mom to court!

The Only Woman to Win the Medal of Honor

Once upon a time, during the tumultuous days of the American Civil War, there lived a remarkable woman named Dr. Mary Edwards Walker. She was not only one of the few female doctors of her time but also a brave soul who would go on to become the only woman ever to receive the prestigious Medal of Honor, the highest military honor in the United States.

Mary Walker was born in 1832 in Oswego, New York, into a progressive family that believed in equal rights for men and women. Inspired by her parents' unconventional beliefs, Mary pursued a career in medicine, a field dominated by men, and graduated with a medical degree—an extraordinary achievement for a woman in the mid-19th century.

When the Civil War broke out in 1861, Dr. Walker was determined to serve her country and help the wounded soldiers. She volunteered as a surgeon, but the Army initially refused to hire her because she was a woman. Undeterred, Mary worked as a volunteer nurse until she was finally employed as a contract surgeon, one of the very first female surgeons in the US Army.

Dr. Walker was known for her tenacity and dedication. She often crossed battle lines to treat civilians and was not afraid to stand up for what she believed in, including wearing pants instead of a dress, which was highly unusual and controversial at the time.

Her insistence on wearing trousers was practical for her work and a statement of her staunch support for women's rights.

In 1864, while serving at a battlefield in Tennessee, Dr. Walker was captured by Confederate forces. Accused of being a spy, she was imprisoned for several months before being released in a prisoner exchange. Despite this harrowing experience, she continued her medical work until the war ended.

For her bravery, unwavering commitment to her patients, and her groundbreaking role as a female surgeon, Dr. Mary Walker was awarded the Medal of Honor in 1865 by President Andrew Johnson. She remains the only woman to have received this honor. In 1917, her medal was revoked as part of a government review that aimed to tighten the award criteria, but she refused to give it back and wore it proudly until her death. In a fitting tribute to her legacy, her Medal of Honor was officially reinstated by President Jimmy Carter in 1977.

Dr. Mary Walker's story is a powerful reminder of the strength and courage one person can exhibit in the face of adversity. Her life challenges us to fight for what we believe in and to break down barriers, no matter how daunting they may seem. She remains a symbol of heroism and a pioneer for women in medicine and the military.

From Slavery to the Halls of Congress

In the tapestry of American history, filled with tales of courage and transformation, the story of Robert Smalls stands out as one of the most remarkable. Born into slavery in 1839 in Beaufort, South Carolina, Smalls would go on to defy the bounds of his enslavement in a daring escape, and rise to become a U.S. Congressman, shaping the very fabric of the nation he once served as a slave.

Robert Smalls' journey to freedom is a thrilling tale of bravery and cleverness. During the Civil War, he was forced to work on the CSS Planter, a Confederate military transport in Charleston harbor. Smalls was an experienced sailor and wheelman, skills that would soon serve him in an extraordinary way. On May 13, 1862, seizing a remarkable opportunity, Smalls executed a daring plan. While the white crew members were onshore, he and several other enslaved crewmen commandeered the Planter. Disguising himself as the captain, Smalls navigated the ship past the Confederate forts guarding the harbor, using the secret signals he had learned while observing the captain.

As dawn broke, Smalls steered the ship to the Union blockade, flying a white sheet as a surrender flag. His act not only secured the freedom of the 17 people aboard, including his own family but also provided the Union with valuable intelligence and a significant military asset. Smalls' heroics made him a hero in the North and a symbol of bravery and freedom.

After the war, Smalls capitalized on his stature as a war hero to launch a political career during the Reconstruction era, a period when the United States grappled with how to rebuild and integrate the Southern states. Smalls was elected to the South Carolina State Assembly and later to the State Senate, where he fought tirelessly for legislation that advanced civil rights, including the creation of the first free and compulsory public school system in the United States.

His commitment to equality and justice propelled him further, and he was elected to the United States House of Representatives. During his tenure in Congress, Smalls advocated for the rights of African Americans across the South, pushing for legislation to integrate the U.S. military and ensure equal rights under the law.

Robert Smalls' life from slavery to Congress embodies the potential for change and highlights the profound impact one courageous individual can have on the course of history. His legacy teaches us about resilience, the power of seizing opportunities, and the enduring fight for justice. Smalls didn't just escape from slavery; he fought throughout his life to dismantle it, ensuring a better future for generations to come. His story is a testament to the belief that from the depths of hardship and injustice can rise a beacon of hope and change.

Lifelong House Arrest For Conducting Science

Once upon a time in Italy, there lived a brilliant man named Galileo Galilei. Born in Pisa in 1564, Galileo was destined to change the way we look at the sky and understand our place in the universe. His curiosity, intelligence, and inventive spirit led him to become one of the most influential figures in the history of science.

Galileo's journey into the stars began with his fascination with mathematics and natural philosophy. He was a professor of mathematics and was known for his dynamic lectures and inventive experiments. But it was his interest in astronomy that would earn him the title of "The Father of Observational Astronomy."

In 1609, Galileo heard about a new invention from the Netherlands called the "spyglass," which could make distant objects appear closer. Excited by its potential, he quickly improved upon the design and created the first true telescope. With this powerful new tool, Galileo turned his gaze to the heavens, and what he saw changed everything.

Through his telescope, Galileo observed mountains and craters on the moon, proving that it wasn't a smooth, perfect sphere as previously thought. He saw the phases of Venus, which supported the revolutionary idea that planets orbit the sun, not the Earth. Perhaps most famously, he discovered four moons orbiting Jupiter, which he named the Medicean stars, after his patrons.

These observations provided strong support for the heliocentric model of the solar system, proposed by Copernicus, which placed the Sun, not the Earth, at the center.

Galileo's discoveries thrilled some but alarmed others, especially those in the Catholic Church, who held that the Earth was the center of the universe. In 1616, the Church warned Galileo not to support the heliocentric model, but Galileo was not a man to be easily silenced. In 1632, he published his "Dialogue Concerning the Two Chief World Systems," which laid out arguments for both the heliocentric and geocentric models but clearly favored the former.

This publication led to accusations of heresy, and in 1633, Galileo was tried by the Roman Inquisition. Despite his brilliant defense, he was forced to recant his support for heliocentrism and spent the rest of his life under house arrest. During these final years, Galileo continued to work, writing "Two New Sciences," a groundbreaking work in the field of physics.

Galileo's story is one of incredible discovery, passionate curiosity, and the clash between science and dogmatic belief. He laid the foundations for modern physics and astronomy, and his courage in the face of adversity has inspired generations. Galileo taught us to look up and question what we see, and his legacy continues to influence our understanding of the universe to this day.

Why You Don't Want To Be A Male Mantis

In the fascinating and often perilous world of insects, few creatures have a courtship as risky as the male praying mantis. While these insects are known for their tranquil praying stance and their helpful appetite for pests, the male mantis faces a rather grim prospect when it comes to finding a mate. Let's delve into the life and trials of the male praying mantis, where love can literally cost an arm and a leg—or even a head!

Male praying mantises are considerably smaller than their female counterparts and are typically on a mission to find a mate, especially during the mating season. However, this quest for love comes with a high-stakes twist that seems straight out of a horror story. During or after mating, the female praying mantis has a notorious habit of turning on her partner and eating him!

This gruesome behavior is known as sexual cannibalism, and it's not just a rare horror show in the insect world—it's quite common among praying mantises. Scientists believe that this macabre act provides the female with the necessary nutrients to ensure the health and viability of her eggs. By consuming the male, the female mantis gets a boost of protein and other nutrients, which can be crucial for the successful development of her offspring.

So, why would the male mantis participate in such a deadly dance? It turns out that nature has equipped these insects with instincts strong enough to drive them towards reproduction, despite the potential cost to their own lives. The drive to pass on their genes is so powerful that male mantises often approach females with great caution, sometimes even attempting to mate from behind to avoid detection and delay their inevitable doom.

For the male praying mantis, mating is quite literally a leap of faith, with each encounter potentially ending in sacrifice. This bizarre reproductive strategy highlights the brutal and often strange ways that different species ensure their survival and pass on their genes to the next generation.

While it's a tough break for the male praying mantis, this strange and dangerous mating ritual reminds us of the incredible diversity and complexity of life on Earth. It serves as a fascinating example of the extreme lengths to which nature will go to ensure that life continues, even at the cost of individual sacrifice. So, the next time you spot a praying mantis gracefully moving or quietly meditating in your garden, spare a thought for the perilous life of the male mantis, whose search for love might just be his last.

The Mysterious Fall of the Roman Empire

Once upon a time, the Roman Empire was the most powerful civilization in the ancient world, with its vast territories spanning Europe, North Africa, and the Middle East. This mighty empire, known for its formidable armies, remarkable engineering, and complex legal systems, seemed invincible. Yet, over time, it experienced a dramatic decline, leading to its mysterious and intriguing fall in 476 AD when the last Roman emperor of the West was deposed.

The fall of the Roman Empire is a tale filled with intrigue, conflict, and multiple factors that chipped away at its foundations. Unlike many empires whose demise can often be pinpointed to a single cause, Rome's fall was the result of a combination of internal weaknesses and external pressures that accumulated over several centuries.

One of the primary internal factors was the political instability that plagued the empire. The Roman government went through numerous changes in leadership and structure, leading to a weakening of authority. Corruption became rampant, and the loyalty of the Roman legions wavered as allegiance to the empire was often replaced by loyalty to commanders who promised wealth and positions of power.

Economically, the empire struggled under the weight of its own massive size. Managing the resources and logistics across the vast territories became increasingly difficult.

Heavy taxes were imposed to support the immense army and bureaucracy, leading to widespread dissatisfaction and economic decline. Additionally, Rome faced serious labor shortages due to reliance on slave labor, which slowed as the number of military conquests declined.

Social decay also contributed to the empire's vulnerabilities. The gap between the rich and poor widened, causing social strife and economic difficulties for the common people. The moral and civic virtue, which had been strong pillars of Roman culture, gradually eroded, replaced by a decline in work ethic and civic participation.

Externally, the empire faced relentless pressure from various groups on the frontiers. These groups, often referred to as "barbarians" by the Romans, included the Goths, Vandals, Huns, and eventually the Franks. These tribes pushed against Rome's borders, driven by various pressures such as migration, displacement by other tribes, and the lure of Rome's wealth.

The introduction and spread of Christianity also played a complex role. As Christianity became more prominent and eventually the state religion, it transformed many aspects of Roman culture and society. Some historians argue that this shift contributed to the empire's decline by undermining the traditional Roman values and diverting focus from civic duty towards a more spiritual outlook.

In 476 AD, the last Roman emperor of the West, Romulus Augustulus, was overthrown by a Germanic leader named Odoacer, marking the traditional date for the fall of the Roman Empire. This event symbolized the end of ancient Rome's dominance and the beginning of the Middle Ages in Europe.

The fall of the Roman Empire remains a powerful story of how even the mightiest empires can decline, reminding us of the importance of good governance, economic stability, and cultural cohesion. It is a narrative that continues to fascinate historians and scholars, serving as a poignant lesson on the complexities of societal endurance and change.

The Taos Hum: A Mysterious Sound in the Desert

In the small, picturesque town of Taos in New Mexico, a peculiar mystery has puzzled residents and visitors for decades. It's known as the Taos Hum—a low, persistent hum or droning sound that can be heard in and around the area. This strange phenomenon has captured the curiosity of many, leading to various investigations and theories about its origin.

The Taos Hum isn't loud, but it is relentless. People who hear it describe a low-frequency sound, similar to a distant diesel engine idling or faint rumbling. Not everyone can hear it, and among those who do, the hum can be a minor nuisance or a major disruption to daily life. Some sensitive hearers report difficulty sleeping or concentrating due to the persistent noise.

The hum was first reported in the early 1990s, though similar sounds have been reported in other parts of the world. The residents of Taos started to discuss the noise among themselves and with local authorities, which led to more widespread knowledge and concern about the phenomenon.

Curious about this auditory anomaly, researchers from various fields including acoustics, geology, and psychology, have studied the Taos Hum. Teams from major institutions like the University of New Mexico have conducted investigations to pinpoint its source, but the hum's origin remains elusive. Several theories have been proposed:

1. **Industrial Equipment:** Some suggest that the hum could be the result of low-frequency noise from industrial machinery or equipment, though no specific sources have consistently been identified.
2. **Electromagnetic Fields:** Another hypothesis is that particular electromagnetic fields produced by power lines or communications devices might be responsible.
3. **Geophysical Phenomenon:** The area's unique geology might amplify or generate low-frequency sounds. Some researchers have speculated that seismic activity could be a contributing factor.
4. **Biological Sources:** There's also the possibility that the hum is a form of tinnitus, an internal perception of sound that can be triggered by auditory or neurological factors.

Despite extensive research, the exact cause of the Taos Hum has not been definitively identified, and it continues to be a subject of both scientific study and local folklore.

For those who hear it, the Taos Hum is more than just a curiosity—it can be a real disturbance. Some residents find the noise so bothersome that they have moved away in search of relief. The hum has also attracted tourists and curiosity seekers to Taos, adding to the town's eclectic charm.

Like other unexplained phenomena, the Taos Hum fuels the imagination and invites a host of questions about the nature of sound and human perception. Whether it's a natural phenomenon, a psychological occurrence, or something else entirely, the mystery of the Taos Hum adds an intriguing layer to the cultural and scientific landscape of this New Mexican town. For now, the hum remains one of the many mysteries that remind us how much remains to be understood about our world.

The Sweet but Sticky Disaster: The Great Molasses Flood

In 1919, a truly unusual and sticky disaster occurred in Boston, Massachusetts, known as the Great Molasses Flood. It might sound like something out of a wacky cartoon, but this was real, and it was no laughing matter for the people who experienced it.

It all started at a storage tank holding over 2 million gallons of molasses, which is a thick, sweet syrup often used in baking and for making candy. The tank was in the North End neighborhood of Boston, and the molasses was there to be used in making rum and other products. But on a chilly January day, something went terribly wrong.

Without warning, the tank suddenly burst, and a massive wave of molasses rushed out. Imagine a giant wall of sticky, sweet syrup, about 25 feet high and moving at 35 miles per hour! The streets of Boston were quickly flooded with molasses, engulfing everything in its path. The force was so strong that it could rip buildings from their foundations and toss them around like toys.

People, horses, and even cars were caught in the flow. The molasses was so thick and sticky that once it caught you, it was almost impossible to escape. Rescue workers struggled to reach people through the sticky mess, and it took days to clean up the affected areas. The flood caused enormous damage and tragically took the lives of 21 people, with many more injured.

So, why did this bizarre disaster happen? Investigators found that the tank had been poorly built and was not strong enough to hold all that molasses, especially when it was filled to the top. The cold temperature on that day also likely contributed, as it made the molasses even thicker and harder to flow, putting extra pressure on the tank.

The Great Molasses Flood taught important lessons about building safety and regulations. After the flood, laws were changed to ensure that such storage tanks were constructed more safely, to prevent anything like this from happening again.

The story of the Great Molasses Flood is a reminder of how unexpected life can be and how even something as harmless as molasses can become dangerous under the right conditions. It's a tale that has stuck in the memory of Boston and is a sweet but solemn note in the city's history.

The Unkillable Soldier

In the annals of military history, few figures embody the spirit of indomitability and courage quite like Sir Adrian Carton de Wiart. His life reads like a script from an action-packed war movie, filled with unbelievable tales of bravery, survival, and an almost comical disregard for danger. Sir Adrian's adventures spanned several decades and wars, earning him a reputation as one of the toughest and most fearless soldiers of his time.

Born in 1880 in Brussels, Belgium, to a Belgian aristocrat and an Irish mother, Adrian Carton de Wiart found himself moving to Britain in his youth. He was drawn to the military early in life, and his career began with the Boer War in South Africa, but it was during World War I and World War II that his legendary status was cemented.

Carton de Wiart participated in the First World War, serving on the Western Front. Throughout his service, he demonstrated a penchant for frontline combat that was extraordinary even by the standards of that brutal war. His exploits included surviving multiple injuries; he was shot in the face, head, stomach, ankle, leg, hip, and ear. In one of the more drastic episodes, he tore off his own fingers when a doctor refused to amputate them. His injuries resulted in him losing his left hand and part of his ear, but not his spirit.

For his valor, he was awarded the Victoria Cross, Britain's highest award for bravery in the face of the enemy. His citation noted his heroism during an attack on an enemy position, citing his exemplary courage despite being severely wounded.

Between the wars, Carton de Wiart served in various positions, including a stint in Poland as a military advisor. However, with the outbreak of World War II, he once again found himself in action. He was sent to Norway to lead the British Military Mission but was soon in the thick of combat during the German invasion of Norway.

Perhaps one of his most famous escapades occurred when he was assigned to lead a mission to Yugoslavia. His aircraft was shot down over the Mediterranean Sea, leading to his capture by Italian forces. Even as a prisoner of war, Carton de Wiart's audacity knew no bounds. He made numerous escape attempts, one of which saw him evading capture for eight days despite being in his sixties.

After his release during a prisoner exchange in 1943, Sir Adrian continued to serve, this time heading to China as Winston Churchill's personal representative. After the war, he retired to Ireland, where he spent his remaining years fishing and recounting his adventures.

Sir Adrian Carton de Wiart's life story is a testament to his unbreakable will and zest for life. His autobiography fittingly titled "Happy Odyssey," captures the undying spirit of a man who not only survived some of the deadliest conflicts in history but did so with an unyielding enthusiasm for action. His story continues to inspire those who hear it, a reminder of the resilience and steadfast courage that define the best of military heroes.

The Exploding Whale: A Blubber Blast from the Past

Once upon a time in the coastal town of Florence, Oregon, a truly bizarre and unforgettable event unfolded—a whale exploded. Yes, you heard that right! In November 1970, what started as a problem of how to dispose of a massive, deceased sperm whale, turned into an explosive tale that would go down in history and become an internet sensation decades later.

The story began when a 45-foot, eight-ton sperm whale washed ashore on the Oregon coast. Normally, the remains of such a giant creature would be left to decompose naturally. However, the whale ended up beached near a populated area on the beach, causing a rather smelly and unsightly dilemma. As it started to decompose, the situation quickly became a public health concern. The overwhelming stench and the possibility of the carcass attracting predators made it imperative for the local authorities to find a solution—and fast.

Enter the Oregon Highway Division, now known as the Oregon Department of Transportation. After considering several options, they decided on an approach that was as drastic as it was dramatic: they would blow up the whale with dynamite. The idea was that the explosion would disintegrate the whale's remains into smaller pieces, which scavengers would then clean up, solving the problem quickly and efficiently.

The plan was set into motion. With half a ton of dynamite in tow, the highway engineers placed the explosives on the leeward side of the whale, hoping to blast the carcass towards the ocean. Spectators gathered, media cameras rolled, and the fuse was lit, everyone eager to see the outcome of this unusual solution.

However, the explosion didn't go quite as planned. Instead of obliterating the whale into manageable pieces, the dynamite charge caused large chunks of blubber to fly through the air. Enormous pieces of whale flesh rained down on the surrounding area, damaging property and smashing a car parked more than a quarter of a mile away. Thankfully, no one was injured, but the event left the beach messier than before, with much of the whale still intact.

The exploding whale incident quickly became legendary, serving as a cautionary tale about the perils of misjudging the use of explosives. It also highlighted the unexpected challenges that can arise in managing nature and wildlife. In the years that followed, the story was frequently shared and embellished, becoming a staple of bizarre local lore. In the digital age, the exploding whale found new life on the internet, captivating audiences worldwide with footage of the explosion.

Today, the tale of the exploding whale remains a fascinating snapshot of a moment when human ingenuity, wildlife management, and explosive materials collided—literally. It's a reminder of nature's scale and unpredictability, and of the sometimes explosive consequences of human intervention.

The Symphony of a Genius

Once upon a time in the classical city of Bonn, Germany, a boy was born who would grow to shake the foundations of music with his genius. Ludwig van Beethoven, born in December 1770, embarked on a musical journey that not only defined his life but also left an indelible mark on the world of Western music.

From a young age, Beethoven was immersed in music, trained by his father Johann and other local musicians. His father, recognizing early the boy's potential, was a strict and demanding teacher. Despite the harsh methods, Beethoven's talent was undeniable, and by his teenage years, he was already a notable organist and harpsichordist in Bonn.

In his early twenties, Beethoven moved to Vienna, which was then the heart of the musical world. Vienna was the place where composers like Mozart and Haydn had set the stage, and it was here that Beethoven planned to compose his own symphonies. Initially, he gained renown as a brilliant pianist and composer of piano music. His early works won him patrons and admirers, but it was his unique approach to composition that set him apart.

As Beethoven's career progressed, he began to experiment and innovate in ways that no one before him had dared. His compositions broke the norms of classical music, introducing new structures and emotional depth that were unprecedented. Works such as his Third Symphony ("Eroica") and the Ninth Symphony ("Choral") pushed musical boundaries and challenged audiences.

His music became synonymous with the shift from the Classical to the Romantic era in music, characterized by its expressiveness and the use of music to convey a narrative or express deep emotions.

However, Beethoven's life was not without its struggles. In his late twenties, he began to lose his hearing, a devastating fate for a musician. By the time he composed some of his greatest works, including the latter symphonies and the celebrated "Fidelio" opera, he was almost completely deaf. Despite this incredible challenge, Beethoven's determination to compose was unshaken. He adapted by using conversation books to communicate and reportedly cutting the legs off his piano to feel the vibrations of the notes through the floor.

Beethoven's personal life was marked by difficulties, including a tumultuous family life and unfulfilled romantic relationships. His relationship with his nephew Karl was particularly strained and brought him significant personal distress. Despite these challenges, Beethoven's commitment to his art never wavered.

When Beethoven passed away in 1827, thousands gathered in Vienna to pay homage to the man who had redefined what music could be. His legacy was that of a revolutionary artist whose compositions heralded a new era of music that expressed the complexities of human emotion and the beauty of nature.

Beethoven's life reminds us that the human spirit can overcome tremendous obstacles and that true creativity often comes from facing and overcoming adversities. His symphonies and sonatas continue to inspire musicians and music lovers around the world, a testament to his enduring genius and the universal language of music.

The King with Six Queens: The Turbulent Marriages of Henry VIII

Once upon a time in England, there reigned a king who was famous not just for his rule but for his many wives. King Henry VIII, a monarch of ambition and grandeur, married six times throughout his reign, each marriage making its own unique mark on history. This tale of love, betrayal, power, and tragedy unfolds like a dramatic play, each act closing with a new queen and a new fate.

Henry VIII ascended to the throne in 1509, full of promise and vigor. He was not only a charismatic and handsome young king but also a scholar and a sportsman. His first marriage was to Catherine of Aragon, a Spanish princess. They were married for nearly 24 years, a union initially marked by affection but shadowed by a lack of a male heir. Catherine bore Henry six children, but tragically, only one, Mary, survived infancy. Desperate for a male successor to secure his dynasty, Henry sought to annul his marriage to Catherine, setting the stage for a historical break with the Catholic Church.

When the Pope refused to annul his marriage, Henry's determination led to the English Reformation. He established the Church of England, appointing himself as its supreme head and granted his own annulment. He then married Anne Boleyn in 1533, a union that promised hope but ended in scandal. Anne gave birth to Elizabeth, the future queen, but failed to produce a male heir. Accused of high treason, Anne was executed in 1536, marking a gruesome end to Henry's most controversial marriage.

Merely days after Anne's execution, Henry married Jane Seymour, who was widely considered his favorite wife because she gave birth to Henry's long-desired male heir, Edward. Tragically, Jane died shortly after childbirth, leaving Henry devastated.

Henry's pursuit of happiness and stability led him to marry three more times. Anne of Cleves was his fourth wife, chosen based on her portraits. However, their marriage was short-lived as Henry found no attraction to her upon their first meeting, leading to another annulment. His fifth wife, Catherine Howard, was young and vivacious, but her alleged infidelity led to her execution. Lastly, Catherine Parr, his sixth wife, outlived Henry. She was a compassionate nurse to him in his obese and ill health and a reformer in her own right.

Henry's matrimonial ventures dramatically shaped England's political landscape, influencing international alliances and religious transformations. Each queen played a role in the cultural and political fabric of Tudor England, from fostering the Protestant Reformation to solidifying new political alliances across Europe.

The story of Henry VIII and his six queens is not just a tale of marital discord but a saga of power, reform, and legacy. It highlights the absolute power of the monarchy and the vulnerable position of queenship in the turbulent waters of Tudor politics. Today, the tales of Henry and his wives continue to captivate people around the world, reminding us of the human stories behind the grand facade of history.

The Multiple Moon Theory

Once upon a time, our planet Earth may have danced with more than just one moon in the night sky. This intriguing theory, proposed by some scientists, suggests that long ago, Earth might have had additional, smaller moons that have since disappeared or merged with the moon we know today. This scenario opens up a fascinating chapter in the story of our planet's cosmic ballet and offers a glimpse into the complex and dynamic processes that have shaped our solar system.

The multiple moon theory is based on computer simulations and geological evidence from the moon itself. According to this theory, shortly after the formation of the Earth, about 4.5 billion years ago, our planet was struck by a Mars-sized object. This colossal collision is believed to have thrown vast amounts of debris into orbit around Earth, which eventually coalesced to form the moon. However, some scientists speculate that not all the debris from this event merged into a single satellite. Instead, some of it might have formed one or more smaller moons.

These hypothetical additional moons would have orbited Earth alongside our current moon. Over time, gravitational interactions between these moons could have led to a variety of outcomes. One possibility is that the smaller moons eventually crashed into the larger moon, leaving behind geological traces that can still be seen today. Another possibility is that they might have collided back into the Earth or were ejected from Earth's orbit entirely, lost to the depths of space.

One piece of evidence that supports this theory comes from the strange asymmetry of the moon's surface. The moon's far side has a much thicker crust than the side facing Earth, which some scientists argue could be the result of a smaller moon having impacted the far side, creating additional layers of material.

Moreover, the theory helps explain some of the peculiarities in the moon's geological composition and anomalies in its orbital dynamics that are difficult to account for under the single moon formation scenario. For example, the differences in isotopic compositions between Earth and the moon suggest a more complex narrative of their early relationship and formation.

While the multiple moon theory is not widely accepted and remains highly speculative, it adds a layer of mystery and wonder to our understanding of Earth's celestial companions. It reminds us that the history of our planet and its moon might be more complicated and intertwined than we currently comprehend.

As we continue to explore our moon and others in our solar system, each discovery brings us closer to unraveling the secrets of our cosmic neighborhood. Whether Earth once had multiple moons or not, this theory encourages us to look up at the night sky with a sense of curiosity and marvel at the potential stories that await discovery.

The Colorful History of Carrots: From Purple to Orange

Believe it or not, the bright orange carrots we know and love today haven't always been orange. In fact, the journey of the carrot through history is a vibrant tale of agriculture, politics, and art that paints a picture of how humans can influence the development of a vegetable. Originally, carrots grown in the wild over 1,000 years ago were typically purple or white with a thin, forked root. But it was the domestication and selective breeding of this humble root vegetable that brought about the wide array of colors we see today, including the predominant orange.

The story begins in Central Asia, specifically in the area that is now Afghanistan. This region is where purple, white, and yellow carrots were originally cultivated. These early carrots were quite different from the ones we eat today, being more fibrous and less sweet. As trade routes expanded, carrots began to spread to other parts of Asia, and eventually into the Middle East and North Africa.

It was in these new lands that the carrot began to change. Agriculturalists in the Middle East cultivated these colorful roots into something bigger and tastier. By the 10th century, the purple and yellow carrots were quite common in the region. The variety of colors in carrots grew as they were introduced to new lands, including red and white ones that appeared through natural mutations and selective breeding.

However, the orange carrot that we are most familiar with today didn't make its appearance until the 16th and 17th centuries in the Netherlands. According to popular legend, Dutch growers cultivated orange carrots as a tribute to William of Orange, who led the struggle for Dutch independence. Though this story might be apocryphal, the development of the sweet, orange root vegetable we know now certainly became especially popular in the Netherlands. Dutch farmers are credited with developing this orange carrot by selecting and planting seeds from the yellowest carrots, eventually stabilizing the mutation into the bright orange variety that dominated the world market.

This carrot was not only more palatable but also had a robust shape that made it easier to grow and more appealing to eat. The orange carrot quickly became the most popular variety, and it is the one that has been selectively bred into the sweet, large, non-forked carrots that we eat today.

Today, you can still find carrots in a multitude of colors, from purple to yellow to red, especially at farmers' markets or in heirloom seed catalogs. These colors are not just visually striking but are also a testament to the carrot's long genetic journey influenced by human hands.

So next time you crunch into a crisp, orange carrot, remember that it's not just a vegetable but a historical artifact that has evolved through centuries of agriculture and human preference, from the purple roots of Central Asia to the orange delights in our salads and stews today!

The Secrets of Stonehenge

Imagine a huge circle of giant stones standing in the middle of a grassy field. This isn't just any circle, but Stonehenge, one of the most famous and mysterious places in the world! Located in England, Stonehenge has puzzled people for thousands of years. Who built it? How did they do it? And most importantly, why? Let's dig into the secrets of Stonehenge and see if we can uncover some of its mysteries!

What is Stonehenge?

Stonehenge is made up of big stones arranged in a circle. Some of these stones are as tall as 30 feet—that's as tall as two giraffes stacked on top of each other! These stones are really heavy too, some weighing as much as 25 tons (that's like five big elephants!). What makes it even more amazing is that these stones were placed there a very, very long time ago —about 5,000 years ago, during a time we call the Neolithic period.

How Was Stonehenge Built?

The big question everyone asks is, "How did people so long ago move such huge stones?" Well, scientists think they might have dragged them over the land using sledges and rollers made from tree trunks. It's like how you might build a sandcastle on the beach, but imagine your sand buckets are super heavy rocks!

The stones came from different places. Some of the smaller ones, called bluestones, came from Wales, which is over 140 miles away. Imagine dragging a heavy stone longer than a marathon race! The larger sandstone blocks, known as sarsens, likely came from closer by, but they were still really heavy and hard to move.

Why Was Stonehenge Built?

Now, here's where it gets even more interesting! Why did people build Stonehenge? There are a lot of ideas, but no one knows for sure. Some people think it was a place for ancient ceremonies or celebrations. Maybe it was like a giant calendar! During the summer and winter solstices (the longest and shortest days of the year), the sun lines up perfectly with some of the stones, which makes many believe it was used to mark special times of the year.

Others think it might have been a special burial ground or a place to remember and honor people from long ago, kind of like a graveyard but much fancier.

Stonehenge Today

Today, Stonehenge is still standing, and it's a big mystery that people from all over the world come to see. It's protected so that it won't get damaged, and many scientists and archaeologists (those are people who study old things made by humans) are still trying to learn its secrets.

So, the next time you see a circle of stones, whether it's small pebbles in your backyard or a big arrangement like Stonehenge, think about how for thousands of years, people have been using stones to tell stories, mark places, and maybe even celebrate big events. And who knows? Maybe one day, you'll help solve the mystery of why Stonehenge was really built!

The Epic Race to the South Pole

In the early 20th century, a gripping drama of exploration unfolded in the icy realms of Antarctica. This was the historic race to the South Pole, a daring contest between two intrepid adventurers: Roald Amundsen from Norway and Robert Falcon Scott from Britain. Their expeditions, marked by both triumph and tragedy, encapsulated the heroic age of Antarctic exploration and left a lasting legacy on how we view human endurance and the quest for knowledge under extreme conditions.

Roald Amundsen, originally planning to conquer the North Pole, switched his focus to the South Pole upon hearing that both Frederick Cook and Robert Peary claimed to have reached the North Pole. Amundsen aimed for the South instead, keeping his plans secret until the last moment. In contrast, Robert Falcon Scott had been planning his journey back to the Antarctic, following a previous expedition that had brought him close to the Pole. Scott's mission was as much scientific as it was geographical, aiming to conduct extensive scientific research along the way.

Amundsen's approach to the expedition was characterized by careful planning, attention to detail, and a singular focus on reaching the Pole. He used skis and dog sleds for rapid movement across the ice, and his team wore practical furs which were better suited to the extreme cold. Amundsen also chose a direct route to the Pole that would save time and energy.

Scott, on the other hand, planned a more complex journey, with motor sledges, ponies, and dogs, most of which did not perform well in the harsh Antarctic conditions. The ponies were particularly unsuited to the icy terrain and cold, and the motor sledges quickly broke down. Eventually, Scott and his men resorted to man-hauling their heavy sleds, which took a tremendous toll on their strength and morale.

On December 14, 1911, Amundsen's expedition reached the South Pole, a full month before Scott. Amundsen's team planted the Norwegian flag at the Pole, achieving the primary goal of their expedition. They returned safely to their base, having successfully navigated the dangerous ice fields without serious injury or loss of life.

Tragically, Scott's expedition did not fare as well. They reached the Pole on January 17, 1912, only to find the Norwegian flag already fluttering in the wind. The devastated team turned back, but the return journey became a deadly battle against exhaustion, starvation, and extreme cold. Scott and his four companions perished on the ice, their bodies found months later, along with Scott's poignant diary.

The race to the South Pole is often remembered not just for the physical accomplishments of these explorers but also for the stark contrast in leadership, preparation, and fate of the two teams. Amundsen's pragmatism and focus on the primary goal led to his success and survival, while Scott's tragic end emphasized the perilous nature of polar exploration and the human cost of reaching the ends of the Earth.

Today, the story of Amundsen and Scott serves as a powerful reminder of the limits of human endurance and the spirit of exploration that drives us to venture into the unknown, regardless of the risks. Their journey to the South Pole remains one of the most dramatic tales in the history of exploration.

The Great Pyramid of Giza: A Marvel of Ancient Engineering

Once upon a time, in the ancient land of Egypt, stood a monument so grand that it would continue to astound humanity for millennia. This is the Great Pyramid of Giza, the oldest and largest of the three pyramids on the Giza plateau and one of the Seven Wonders of the Ancient World. Built as a tomb for the Pharaoh Khufu, also known as Cheops, it is a testament to ancient Egypt's architectural brilliance and enduring mystery.

The Great Pyramid was constructed during Egypt's Fourth Dynasty in the 26th century BC, a time when the kingdom was wealthy and powerful. Khufu, the second pharaoh of this dynasty, commissioned this colossal structure as his gateway to immortality. The pyramid was designed to protect his mummified body and ensure his transformation from earthly king to celestial ruler.

Constructed from millions of limestone blocks, each weighing several tons, the pyramid stands at an original height of 146.6 meters (481 feet), making it the tallest man-made structure in the world for over 3,800 years until the completion of Lincoln Cathedral in England in the 14th century. The precision with which these blocks were cut and assembled remains one of the greatest architectural feats in human history.

The pyramid's construction is believed to have taken about 20 years, a period during which tens of thousands of laborers worked in three-month shifts. Contrary to popular belief, these workers were not slaves but skilled laborers, who were well-fed and housed in nearby workers' camps. The labor force included stone cutters, masons, engineers, and other craftsmen, who meticulously shaped and transported the limestone and granite used in the pyramid's construction.

One of the most intriguing aspects of the Great Pyramid is its complex interior chambers and passageways. The main chambers include the King's Chamber, the Queen's Chamber, and the Grand Gallery. The King's Chamber, located at the heart of the pyramid, houses a granite sarcophagus that was intended for Khufu's mummy, although his body has never been found.

This chamber is accessed via the Grand Gallery, a long, high corridor that is an architectural marvel in itself, showcasing the Egyptians' advanced understanding of weight distribution and interior design.

The construction techniques used to build the Great Pyramid are still not fully understood. Theories suggest that a straight or spiral ramp was used to haul the massive stones into place. Others propose that the blocks were hauled up a mud-slicked slope. Regardless of the methods used, the construction of the Great Pyramid remains one of the most significant achievements of ancient engineering.

The Great Pyramid of Giza not only embodies the organizational prowess of Ancient Egypt but also its spiritual and cultural values. It was part of a larger complex that included two other major pyramids, smaller pyramids for queens, several temples, and a workers' village, which together illustrate a highly sophisticated and interconnected society.

Today, the Great Pyramid continues to be a source of fascination and inspiration, drawing millions of tourists and scholars from around the world. Its enduring allure lies in its mysterious past and the sheer audacity of its construction, a monument built to last an eternity, a fitting homage to the ancient Egyptians' quest for immortality.

The Legendary Escape From Alcatraz

On a foggy night in June 1962, one of the most audacious prison breaks in history unfolded at Alcatraz Federal Penitentiary, a maximum-security facility located on an island in San Francisco Bay. Known as "The Rock," Alcatraz was considered one of the most secure prisons in the world, supposedly escape-proof due to its isolated location and the treacherous currents surrounding it. However, three inmates, Frank Morris, Clarence Anglin, and John Anglin, challenged this claim in a meticulously planned escape that remains shrouded in mystery and intrigue.

Frank Morris, along with brothers Clarence and John Anglin, began their escape plan by exploiting the prison's structural weaknesses. Over the course of several months, they used discarded saw blades, spoons stolen from the cafeteria, and an improvised drill made from a broken vacuum cleaner motor to gradually widen the ventilation ducts in their cells. Behind their cells lay a utility corridor that was unguarded and largely unpatrolled.

To conceal their nightly work, the men crafted false wall segments from cardboard and painted them to look like the surrounding walls. They also created lifelike dummy heads from a mixture of soap, toilet paper, and real human hair, which they placed in their beds to fool the guards during nighttime head counts.

Their preparation extended beyond the physical barriers of their cells. Knowing the treacherous waters around Alcatraz could be lethal, the inmates crafted a raft and life vests from over fifty stolen raincoats, which they fused together using heat from the prison's steam pipes. They also accumulated a small hoard of supplies, including food and water.

On the night of June 11, 1962, after months of preparation, Morris and the Anglin brothers put their plan into action. They squeezed through the holes they had carved in their cell walls, climbed into the utility corridor, and ascended to the prison roof. From there, they shimmied down a drainpipe, climbed over two barbed-wire fences, and launched their makeshift raft into the cold, choppy waters of San Francisco Bay.

The escape triggered one of the most extensive manhunts in history. Despite the efforts of the FBI, Coast Guard, and local law enforcement, the men were never found. Officially, the case was closed in 1979, with the assumption that the escapees drowned, unable to overcome the Bay's strong currents and hypothermia-inducing water temperatures. However, no bodies were ever recovered, leading to speculation and conspiracy theories that they might have survived and assumed new identities.

The 1962 escape from Alcatraz has since entered popular lore, inspiring books, documentaries, and films. It remains a captivating story of human ingenuity and resilience, and continues to be a subject of fascination and debate.

Did Morris and the Anglin brothers perish, or did they manage to pull off one of the most incredible escapes in penal history? The truth remains elusive, much like the men themselves, adding to the legend of Alcatraz and its most famous escape.

The Curse of the Pharaohs

In November 1922, the world was gripped by an incredible archaeological discovery in the Valley of the Kings, Egypt. The British archaeologist Howard Carter unearthed the nearly intact tomb of Tutankhamun, a pharaoh who ruled during Egypt's 18th Dynasty, around 1323 BC. This sensational find not only provided unprecedented insights into ancient Egyptian civilization but also sparked widespread fascination with the rumored "Curse of the Pharaohs" — a supposed hex believed to bring misfortune or death to those who disturbed the resting places of ancient Egyptian royals.

Tutankhamun's tomb was a treasure trove, filled with incredible artifacts meant to accompany the young king into the afterlife. Among the riches were golden shrines, jewelry, sculptures, a chariot, and the iconic golden burial mask that has since become a symbol of ancient Egypt. Unlike many royal tombs, it had been largely untouched by looters, offering a pristine snapshot of ancient Egyptian burial practices and daily life.

However, the wonder and excitement of this historic discovery were soon overshadowed by eerie incidents and untimely deaths, leading to media speculation about a curse. Lord Carnarvon, the financial backer of the excavation team, died less than five months after the tomb's opening.

His death was due to an infected mosquito bite, which he accidentally aggravated, leading to blood poisoning. Newspapers at the time sensationalized this event, suggesting that his death was a result of the pharaoh's curse.

The notion of the curse was fueled by reports that the tomb's entrance bore an inscription that read: "Death shall come on swift wings to him who disturbs the peace of the king." Although this particular inscription was never actually found, various other "curses" alleged to have been found in other tombs were publicized in the press. Adding to the mystique, several other people connected with the discovery died in the years following, under sometimes mysterious circumstances, including Howard Carter's personal secretary and a radiologist who x-rayed Tutankhamun's mummy.

Despite these stories, many experts and scholars argue that the curse is nothing more than a myth, propagated by the media at the time to increase newspaper sales. Moreover, many people associated with the tomb's discovery, including Howard Carter himself, lived long after the event. Carter worked extensively in the tomb for nearly a decade after its opening and lived until 1939 without any supernatural repercussions.

Scientific explanations have also been offered for the alleged curse, including the presence of toxic molds and bacteria in the sealed tombs, which could have caused severe allergic reactions or lung infections in those who inhaled them.

Today, the story of Tutankhamun and the curse of the pharaohs remains one of the most thrilling narratives in the history of archaeology, blending fact with fiction. It serves as a testament to humanity's enduring fascination with ancient cultures and the mysteries of the past. Whether fact or fiction, the legend of the pharaoh's curse continues to captivate the imaginations of historians, adventurers, and the public alike.

Two Boys Find an Incredible Treasure

In 1978, a remarkable discovery unfolded on a quiet farm in Silverdale, England, transforming an ordinary day into an extraordinary moment in the history of archaeology. This was the day when two young boys, exploring the grounds of their family farm, stumbled upon one of the most significant Viking treasures ever found in Britain. This discovery, later known as the Silverdale Hoard, would capture the imagination of historians and treasure seekers alike, shedding light on the rich and tumultuous period of the Viking presence in England.

The adventure began when the boys, simply hoping to find something interesting buried in the soil, started digging. To their astonishment, they unearthed a lead container filled with silver. Inside, there were over 200 items, including coins, jewelry, ingots, and other precious objects. Among the trove were beautifully crafted silver arm rings and necklaces, each piece telling a story of craftsmanship and trade from over a millennium ago.

What made the Silverdale Hoard particularly significant was its composition and the clues it held about the Viking era. The hoard contained a mix of coinage from different regions, including Northumbria and other parts of the Viking world, indicating the extensive reach of Viking trade networks. Additionally, the presence of hack silver—pieces of cut and bent silver—suggested that the Vikings used silver not just for ornamentation but also as a form of currency and social status.

The coins found in the hoard were especially telling. They dated back to around the 9th century, a time when the Vikings were not only raiders but also settlers who had begun to establish their own territories in England. Some of the coins bore the names of lesser-known Viking kings, providing historians with invaluable information about the political landscape of the time.

The discovery of the Silverdale Hoard not only provided a snapshot of Viking life but also highlighted the complexities of their interactions with the local populations. It suggested a degree of integration and adaptation by the Vikings into local cultures, seen through the blending of art styles and economic systems.

Following the discovery, the hoard was declared a treasure trove, meaning it was considered property of the Crown according to British law, designed to protect archaeological artifacts. The boys' find was promptly reported, and the artifacts were taken for conservation and detailed study. Today, many of these items are on display in museums, where they continue to educate and fascinate visitors about the Viking age.

The story of the Silverdale Hoard is a testament to the unpredictability and excitement of archaeological discovery. It underscores the idea that history is often just below our feet, waiting to be uncovered by those curious enough to dig a little deeper. For the two young boys on that farm in Silverdale, their adventurous spirit led to a find that enriched our understanding of history, proving that sometimes, the greatest treasures are found in the most unexpected places.

The Explorer Who Redrew the World Map

In the late 15th century, an ambitious navigator embarked on a voyage that would forever change the course of history. This explorer was Christopher Columbus, a man whose intrepid journeys across the Atlantic Ocean played a pivotal role in reshaping the world map and initiating the era of global exploration.

Born in Genoa, Italy, around 1451, Columbus grew up amidst the stories of mariners, which likely sparked his deep interest in ocean voyages. As he matured into a skilled navigator, Columbus developed a bold theory: he believed that sailing west across the Atlantic would be a quicker route to the rich spice islands of Asia, known then as the Indies. At that time, the conventional trade routes to Asia were long and perilous, traveling over land or around the southern tip of Africa.

Fueled by this idea, Columbus sought support for his expedition from several European monarchs, facing rejection multiple times. Finally, Spain's Queen Isabella I and King Ferdinand II agreed to sponsor his journey. They were motivated by the potential of gaining a competitive edge over other European powers by discovering new trade routes.

On August 3, 1492, Columbus set sail from Palos de la Frontera, Spain, with three ships—the Niña, the Pinta, and the Santa María. After more than two months at sea, on October 12, 1492, land was sighted. This landfall, though he believed it to be Asia, was actually one of the Bahamian islands. Columbus went on to explore parts of the Caribbean, including the islands of Cuba and Hispaniola, still under the impression that he had reached the outskirts of Asia.

Columbus's "discovery" of these lands was monumental because it was unknown to Europeans at that time that two entire continents, later to be known as the Americas, lay to the west of Europe across the Atlantic. This misconception began a series of events that would eventually map these vast new territories, significantly altering Europeans' understanding of world geography.

Columbus made a total of four voyages across the Atlantic Ocean, encountering various indigenous peoples and mapping portions of the Caribbean, Central America, and South America. His expeditions marked the beginning of centuries of transatlantic conquests and colonization, known as the Age of Discovery. However, these voyages also heralded the beginning of widespread European colonization and exploitation of the Americas, which had profound and often devastating impacts on the native populations.

While Columbus did not achieve his original goal of finding a new route to Asia, his journeys played a critical role in opening up the New World to European exploration and colonization. For better or worse, Columbus's voyages redrew the world map, expanding the geographical horizons of the contemporary world and setting the stage for the global interactions of future generations.

Today, Christopher Columbus remains a controversial figure, celebrated by some as an icon of exploration and vilified by others for his role in colonizing new lands and exploiting native peoples. Nonetheless, his legacy as the explorer who redrew the world map is an indelible part of history.

The Cookie Monster Ransom

In a tale that sounds straight out of a whimsical storybook, the Cookie Monster once became an infamous character not just on TV screens but in a real-life drama involving a stolen golden cookie and a ransom note. This quirky incident occurred in January 2013, involving the iconic symbol of the famous German biscuit company, Bahlsen, based in Hanover.

The caper began when a century-old golden cookie, which had proudly adorned the facade of Bahlsen's office, mysteriously disappeared. The city was left puzzled over the fate of this beloved emblem, until a letter addressed to the company and local newspapers revealed the unlikely culprit: someone claiming to be the Cookie Monster from the children's TV show "Sesame Street."

The ransom note was as peculiar as the crime itself. The thief, donning a Cookie Monster costume, sent a photo holding the golden cookie and demanded that Bahlsen provide free cookies to all children in a local hospital. The letter stated that failure to comply would result in the cookie being thrown away. The "Cookie Monster" showed a playful side of villainy, striking a nerve of public amusement rather than fear.

Intrigued and bemused by the unusual nature of this theft, Bahlsen decided to play along. The company announced that it would donate 52,000 packets of cookies to 52 different social institutions if the golden cookie was safely returned, effectively meeting the demands of the "Cookie Monster" in a way that would benefit the community.

Shortly after, the golden cookie mysteriously reappeared, found hanging from the neck of a horse statue of a local university, wrapped carefully in a red ribbon. The cookie was undamaged and soon restored to its rightful place, albeit with increased security.

The true identity of the Cookie Monster thief was never publicly revealed, and the case was eventually closed. The event, however, left a lasting impression, becoming a local legend and a delightful anecdote in the annals of unusual crimes. The Cookie Monster ransom incident is remembered not for malice but for its blend of mischief and whimsy, demonstrating that even in the world of theft, there's room for a touch of humor and a taste for cookies.

Cleopatra's Cockroach Perfume: Myth or Ancient Beauty Secret?

Cleopatra VII, the last active ruler of the Ptolemaic Kingdom of Egypt, is renowned not just for her political acumen but also for her legendary beauty and charm. Among the many tales and speculations about her allure, one peculiar story stands out: the claim that Cleopatra used a perfume made from cockroaches. This intriguing anecdote invites us to explore whether this could be a myth or an actual ancient beauty secret.

Cleopatra's reputation as a seductress and a monarch deeply concerned with her appearance is well-documented in historical texts. She was known to have access to the most exotic and luxurious beauty products of her time, concocted by skilled perfumers and chemists. The Egyptians were pioneers in the creation of perfumes and cosmetics, using a variety of natural ingredients such as flowers, herbs, and oils.

The idea that Cleopatra might have used a cockroach-based perfume, however, is not as far-fetched as it might initially seem. In many ancient cultures, including Egypt, insects were commonly used for medicinal and cosmetic purposes. For example, carmine, a red dye derived from beetles, has been used for millennia as a colorant in cosmetics.

Cockroaches, in particular, were believed to have several beneficial properties. They were used in traditional remedies across various cultures for their supposed health benefits. Some records suggest that ground cockroach paste was used as a treatment for ailments like earaches and indigestion. It is possible that the cockroaches' aromatic potential was also explored in perfumery, given the Egyptians' experimental approach to scents.

However, whether Cleopatra specifically used cockroach perfume is not confirmed by any direct historical evidence. This story could be an embellishment or a misunderstanding of the broader truth that the ancient Egyptians experimented with many unusual ingredients in their quest for the perfect fragrance.

Today, the idea of a cockroach perfume adds a layer of mystique to Cleopatra's already captivating image. It's a reminder of the sophistication of ancient Egyptian culture in their pursuit of beauty and luxury, and of how legends can often blur the lines between historical facts and imaginative interpretations.

Whether myth or reality, the story of Cleopatra's cockroach perfume fascinates us, showcasing the lengths to which historical figures might go to maintain their allure, and the innovative—albeit sometimes strange—cosmetic practices of the past.

The Great Pie Ban: When Eating Pie Was Illegal

Imagine a time when indulging in a slice of pie could land you on the wrong side of the law. This may sound like a quirky tale from a whimsical storybook, but it was once a reality. During the early 17th century in the American colonies, specifically in the Massachusetts Bay Colony, there was a brief period when the simple act of eating pie was indeed against the law.

The ban on pie can be traced back to the Puritans, a religious group known for their strict and somber lifestyle, who were among the early settlers of New England. The Puritans were deeply devout and often suspicious of anything that smacked of excess or indulgence. Their laws and regulations were designed to maintain order, promote sobriety, and uphold their rigorous moral standards.

In 1651, as part of their efforts to quash what they viewed as unnecessary extravagance, the Puritan leaders declared a ban on several luxury items and practices, which they deemed as distractions from religious duties and simple living. Among the banned items and activities were wearing lace and ribbons, drinking in taverns, and yes—eating pie. The Puritans believed that pies, which were often rich and sweet, represented an indulgence that was inconsistent with their values of simplicity and restraint.

The law specifically targeted the making and consuming of pies, as they were seen as a symbol of gluttony. This legal restriction was part of broader "sumptuary laws," which were designed to regulate personal behavior and morality. Sumptuary laws controlled what people could wear, eat, and consume, based on their social rank and moral considerations.

Despite its intentions, the pie ban was not warmly received, nor was it particularly enforceable. Pies were a popular and practical part of the colonial diet, cherished for their ability to preserve food and incorporate whatever fillings were on hand, whether sweet or savory. The backlash from the community was strong enough that the authorities found it difficult to enforce the ban effectively.

The pie prohibition was eventually lifted, and pies returned to their rightful place in the culinary life of the colonies. Today, the episode remains a curious footnote in American history, illustrating the sometimes extreme lengths to which the Puritans were willing to go in order to enforce their moral and religious codes.

The period when eating pie was illegal serves as a reminder of the complex and often surprising ways in which food and morality have intersected throughout history. It underscores how cultural norms and values can shape even the simplest aspects of daily life, including what we eat, and highlights the enduring human love for pie—a dish too delicious to be kept down by law.

The Tunguska Event: The Mystery Blast from the Sky

On a sunny morning in June 1908, a mysterious explosion occurred in the remote wilderness of Siberia near the Tunguska River. This event, now known as the Tunguska Event, remains one of the largest and most baffling impacts in recorded history. With the force of approximately 1,000 Hiroshima bombs, the explosion flattened an estimated 80 million trees over 2,150 square kilometers (830 square miles), creating a shockwave that reverberated around the globe.

The Tunguska Event has captivated scientists, historians, and conspiracy theorists alike, primarily because of the absence of a clear cause and the lack of any identifiable impact crater. At the time, the region was sparsely populated, which, fortunately, meant there were no confirmed human fatalities, though the environmental impact was massive.

Eyewitnesses from the Evenki natives and Russian settlers in the vicinity reported seeing a bluish light, nearly as bright as the sun, moving across the sky followed by a flash and a sound similar to artillery fire. The earth trembled, and a shockwave knocked people off their feet and broke windows hundreds of kilometers away.

For years, the inaccessibility of the area and the political climate in Russia (both during the Tsarist and Communist regimes) delayed scientific expeditions to the Tunguska site. It wasn't until more than a decade later, in 1927, that Soviet scientist Leonid Kulik led a team to conduct the first thorough investigation of the area.

Kulik expected to find a crater from a meteorite impact but instead discovered a region of scorched and flattened trees, radiating outward from a central point in a butterfly pattern. No significant crater was ever found, nor any large fragments of a meteoric body.

The prevailing theory today is that the Tunguska explosion was caused by the airburst of a small comet or a meteoroid about 6 to 10 kilometers (4 to 6 miles) above the Earth's surface. This theory suggests that the cosmic object disintegrated in the atmosphere, releasing enough energy to cause the massive destruction below but evaporating before striking the ground.

Other hypotheses have included everything from a black hole passing through Earth to an alien spaceship crash, though these have little to no scientific evidence to support them. Studies of the area have found microscopic silicate and magnetite spherules in the soil, supporting the meteoroid theory as these could be remnants from the disintegrated alien rock.

The Tunguska Event significantly impacted the scientific community, influencing policies on planetary defense and strategies to deal with potential future threats of cosmic impacts. It sparked an increased interest in the study of meteorites and celestial impacts and their effects on Earth.

The mystery of the Tunguska Event continues to be a popular subject for research and speculation. It serves as a powerful reminder of our planet's vulnerability to cosmic events and the unseen dangers that may lurk in space. Despite over a century of research and exploration, the Tunguska Event retains an air of mystery, securing its place as one of the most intriguing natural phenomena of the twentieth century.

The First Animals In Space

Long before human astronauts ventured into the void of space, our journey to understand the cosmos began with some unlikely pioneers: animals. These early space travelers, including fruit flies, monkeys, dogs, and even cats, played a critical role in shaping the future of space exploration. Their contributions provided essential data about the effects of space travel on living organisms and helped ensure the safety of subsequent human missions.

The very first animals to reach space were fruit flies. In 1947, a group of these tiny insects were placed aboard a U.S.-launched V-2 rocket from White Sands Missile Range in New Mexico. The fruit flies reached an altitude of 68 miles (109 kilometers), crossing the Kármán line that conventionally defines the boundary between Earth's atmosphere and outer space. The flies were chosen because of their well-studied genetics, which scientists hoped would reveal the effects of cosmic radiation. Remarkably, the fruit flies returned to Earth alive and well, providing the first evidence that life could survive the rigors of space travel.

Following the fruit flies, a variety of larger animals began their journeys into space. During the late 1940s and the 1950s, the United States and the Soviet Union initiated programs to send mammals into space. The Soviets focused on dogs, seeing them as suitable for their spaceflight experiments due to their calm demeanor and ability to endure long periods of inactivity.

Perhaps the most famous of these canine cosmonauts was Laika, a stray dog from Moscow, who in 1957 became the first animal to orbit the Earth aboard Sputnik 2. Unfortunately, Laika did not survive the mission, but her legacy was pivotal in advancing human spaceflight.

In the U.S., the space program chose monkeys and apes for their physiological similarities to humans. One of the notable early primate astronauts was Albert I, a rhesus monkey, who flew aboard a V-2 rocket in 1948 but unfortunately died of suffocation during the flight. Subsequent missions improved, and by 1959, Able, a rhesus monkey, and Miss Baker, a squirrel monkey, successfully returned to Earth after traveling in a suborbital flight on a Jupiter rocket.

Cats and rodents also contributed to space exploration. In 1963, France sent the first cat into space, named Félicette. Like many of its predecessors, Félicette was chosen to study the neurological effects of space travel. Equipped with electrodes implanted in her brain, she provided valuable data before being safely recovered. Additionally, mice and rats were frequently used by various countries to study reproduction and development in space.

The use of animals in spaceflight research paved the way for human space travel. Insights gained from these missions contributed to understanding life support and biological responses to weightlessness, radiation, and the stress of launch and reentry. These animal astronauts are remembered as heroes who involuntarily contributed to one of humanity's greatest scientific endeavors.

However, these missions also sparked a significant ethical debate regarding the use of animals in research, particularly in such high-risk environments. The dialogue they initiated continues to influence how we approach scientific experiments involving animals today.

Reflecting on the history of animals in space reminds us of the complexity of our journey to the stars—a journey interwoven with courage, curiosity, and ethical challenges, propelled not just by human ambition but also by the silent contributions of the animal pioneers.

Imprint

MSDKI

195533 N 109th St, Scottsdale, AZ 85255, USA

ISBN: 9798345963203

First Edition

Made in United States
Troutdale, OR
12/03/2024